THE RUDDERHAVEN SCIENCE FICTION AND FANTASY ANTHOLOGY II

Edited by

Douglas Rudder

RudderHaven
3014 Washington Ave
Granite City, IL 62040

Published by:
RudderHaven
3014 Washington Ave
Granite City, IL 62040
USA

First Softcover Printing, July 2014, RudderHaven
(ISBN 978-1-932060-13-3)

Edited by Douglas Rudder, C. K. Deatherage, Sheri Rudder, Becca Rudder
Cover Art and Design: Douglas, Sheri, and Becca Rudder
Nebula image Courtesy NASA/JPL-Caltech
Ireland landscape image Courtesy Jon Sullivan/PDPhoto.org

"The Observer" was previously published in Missing Pieces IV. Old School Publishing, 2013.

Printed in the United States of America

ISBN 978-1-932060-13-3

Acknowledgements

Thanks to all of our authors, editors, and everyone who made this book possible, and to our families and friends for their support and encouragement.

Special thanks to our readers. We hope you enjoy the characters, worlds, and stories we have presented to you. If our stories have sparked your imagination, touched your hearts, or tickled your sense of humor, then we count it a success.

Contents

The Observer

Douglas Rudder

The warehouse district was relatively quiet in the darkness, with only the occasional sound of ground traffic in the distance nearer the heart of the city. It was the middle of the night; most of the surrounding buildings were empty of personnel, except for a scattering of night security. Most normal people were home in bed. The group lurking in the shadowed alleyway was far from normal.

It was an eclectic team gathered in the shadows. Some individuals had a military background, while others were newer to the game, drawn together for a common purpose. All wore black, though there was no distinct uniform. There was a hodge-podge of styles, from rugged combat gear to simple turtlenecks or sweaters.

Their weapons were varied as well. Three of the men sported light assault rifles. Another man, codenamed Longshot, carried a small sniper rifle over his shoulder and a handgun strapped to his hip. The others had handguns of various makes, and a few carried tasers to be used on the security guards. Ideally, there would be no real gunplay, but it was best to be prepared.

I was assigned to the unit to analyze their tactics and capabilities and report my findings to my superiors for inclusion in future training. This particular Resistance cell had been giving OSaR fits; they excelled at sabotage, espionage, and supply raids. The cell was efficient and resourceful, defying the Order at every turn. They knew when and where to strike, always minimizing risks to themselves while reaping the greatest benefit to the remnants of the Earth Defense Force. They were the most successful cell in the Resistance, operating on Earth itself, right in OSaR's seat of power.

At this point, thirteen team members were present. I guess that made me the "lucky number" so to speak, though most of them were not all that pleased with my presence. Their leader, a petite young woman I knew only as "Codecracker," had made that clear during the mission briefing.

Earlier at the assembly area, a mechanics garage that concealed the two panel trucks that would transport us to our destination and carry the cargo from our raid, Codecracker had introduced me to her team. She described my mission briefly, emphasizing afterward that my role was to watch, not interfere.

"Agent Bonner is here as an observer, not a participant." Her blue eyes skewered me with a quick glare. "Apparently the higher ups have been impressed with our results and want to see how we do things. Let's give them a good show. Quick, efficient, and safe. No free-wheeling. We get in, do the job, and go home."

With that, the meeting broke up and the team scattered about the shop to finalize their preparations for the mission. Codecracker walked over to a stack of boxes and picked up a clipboard, going over her checklist with the intensity of a leader who wanted to make sure every contingency was covered, every precaution taken to both accomplish the mission and bring her people home safely.

Yet, even though she exuded leadership and poise, it was also evident that she was not a soldier. Throughout the briefing, she had deferred to other individuals to go over specific parts of the plan. Broadside had handled the tactical overview, Runner discussed transportation, and Bookkeeper went over the wish list for the raid. Codecracker was the coordinator. She had a knack for picking the right people and delegating tasks accordingly. The results were impressive.

Even her appearance indicated that she was a civilian. Her wavy, blonde hair fell short of the shoulders of her close-fitting black sweater. The holster on her hip was small, with an equally small pistol nestled inside. The weapon was lethal enough at close range, but it was obvious that Codecracker was not expected to be a combatant. This, coupled with her choice of codename, implied to me that her expertise was more along the lines of cryptography or intelligence.

I walked over to her, rubbing my throbbing temple and trying not to limp too much on my bad leg—an artifact of my own first encounter with OSaR's shock troops several years earlier. She saw me coming, of course.

Those sharp eyes—and equally sharp mind—didn't miss anything.

"How's the headache?" she asked as I approached.

"I'll live," I responded. The painkiller had not helped. My head was still pounding away, but no use dwelling on it.

"Hopefully we all will." Her eyes locked onto mine. "Look, Agent Bonner, I'm flattered that Command thinks so highly of our work, but I don't like distractions." She poked at my chest, without making contact. "You are a distraction. I don't want my people looking over their shoulders or worrying about making the right impression instead of focusing on the mission. That can get good people killed."

I allowed myself a slight smile. "Crack commando teams don't get distracted, do they?"

She shook her head. "We're not commandos. Look," she said, nodding toward a thin young man in a black sweatshirt, "Bookkeeper is here to run the inventory for us. The woman next to him, Angelheart, is a doctor. Her job is to identify the medications and medical equipment on his list."

Setting her clipboard down on a crate, she gazed around the room at the activity taking place. "The point is, less than half my team even has military experience. The rest are just men and women who want freedom back for their families and friends. The self-proclaimed Order of Science and Reason's vision of a tightly-controlled 'Utopia' is no better than living in a prison camp."

"I understand. No offence intended." I'd seen OSaR's policies in play myself. Those whom Director Rousseau and his Board of Scientists did not deem fit for their interpretation of the perfect Order were often imprisoned, "re-oriented," or even killed. Cold, hard logic was the rule under OSaR. Anything outside their definition was pruned from society.

"Good." Her expression softened a little. "Tonight's run is a straightforward materiel raid. Medical and logistical supplies mainly. The warehouse does not store weapons or explosives, so the security is pretty much standard: A handful of night watchmen, alarm systems, and video surveillance. The systems are accounted for. We have a good chance at getting in and out without too much fanfare."

That conversation ran through my mind as we crouched in the darkness outside the warehouse waiting for the last two members of the team, Pathfinder and Barnstormer, to arrive. Codecracker and her not-commandos saw this as a simple raid. Go in, knock out a few guards, gather the supplies and leave. They did not take it lightly; they were good at what they did.

Unfortunately, I knew something they did not. In addition to the standard complement of night watchmen, there was a half squad of Cyborg troopers stationed at the warehouse. Five "elite" soldiers might not seem like much to some, but the Cyborgs were beyond elite, they were devastating.

Unlike what you might see in vid adventures, OSaR's Cyborgs did not sport robotic appendages or external devices. What they did have were cybernetic implants in their brains, tied into their nervous systems. The nanotechnology involved enhanced all of their bodies' natural function: better resource distribution to bring muscle strength to peak human, faster healing, quicker reflexes, sharper vision, higher intelligence. Not necessarily superhuman, but definitely enhanced.

But the "Technology" OSaR had discovered did more than create physically-enhanced soldiers. The implants allowed the Cyborgs to communicate directly with each other at the speed of thought. Not only that, they could interface wirelessly with any OSaR computer or satellite systems within range, effectively giving them instant tactical information and GPS and tracking capabilities.

In short, the Cyborgs were the most formidable fighting force in the known galaxy. Five of them were waiting for us. And I couldn't tell anyone.

That's right. I knew we were walking into a trap and I had to let it happen. Part of my mission was to see how the Resistance cell would react and adapt to the situation. They had sprung traps before and come out convincingly on top, but to my knowledge they had never faced a foe like this one. This mission would be their ultimate test. The results would be part of my analysis—provided I survived to tell about it.

A double-snap came from the end of the alley where Roach (I never did find out the origin of that codename) was stationed. Moments later Pathfinder and Barnstormer strode silently into view. The two men huddled with Codecracker in whispered conversation. Even though I could not hear what they were saying, their body language betrayed excitement.

Codecracker motioned the rest of us over. We formed a semi-circle around where she knelt on one knee. Her eyes shone with a fiery determination.

"Change in plans. Pathfinder just informed me that this warehouse is system hot."

I could almost sense anticipation ripple through those present. I did not know what "system hot" meant, but the importance was not lost on the others.

"Are we scrapping the materiel raid?" Broadside's low voice rumbled the question on everyone's mind.

"No, we'll go ahead as planned," Codecracker said, waving off the suggestion. She picked out a couple of men with her eyes. "Pathfinder, Dart, you're with me. We'll head for the office while the rest of the team carries out the original mission."

Her expression turned grave as her gaze swept across the raid team. "I don't need to tell you how vital this opportunity is to the war effort. If anything goes wrong, I'm counting on you to help buy us the time we need to get our part done."

The only response was silent assent. I glanced around the group, especially noting the civilians' reactions. There was no fear in their faces; if anything, perhaps a nervous enthusiasm. They clearly knew what was at stake, and were ready to accept the challenge.

I checked the action on my Magnum, dread and determination washing through me. Whatever happened, I was going to do my dead level best to keep Codecracker alive and help her accomplish her new objective—even if it meant disregarding my own orders. Now I had to figure out how to attach myself to her mission instead of the raiders.

I needn't have worried. Codecracker came over to me and said quietly, "Bonner, you come with me."

"If you think I can be of help."

"It's not a matter of helping; I just want to keep you out of my unit's way. No distractions, remember?"

Though her words were harsh, her voice lacked the venom it had earlier. She was looking out for her people, the way any good leader would. I would have done the same in her position.

"You're in charge." I needed to put her mind at ease as far as I was concerned. I wanted to fade into the background and let her focus on her goal.

Codecracker gestured to Broadside. He nodded his acknowledgement and began mobilizing the unit. Barnstormer and two others headed around the wall between the alley and the street across from the target warehouse. I noticed Longshot trot off to the building behind us and start up the fire escape toward the roof. Good move. A sniper on that roof would have a clear field of fire over the loading docks and parking lot, covering the west and south sides of the building.

The rest of us were waiting, ready to move forward when the gate was clear. A faint crackle of electricity sounded near the south gate. A few seconds later it swung silently open and Barnstormer waved us in.

A quick sprint across the street brought us to the gate. Two security guards lay in the corner, securely trussed up, and out of sight of the warehouse. Taser in hand, Barnstormer gave Pathfinder a quick fist bump, then led his two companions across the narrow gap between the gate and a small outbuilding to seek out the next set of guards patrolling the fence line. That brief show of camaraderie reminded me of my own time in the Earth Defense Force. That was long ago, before OSaR came into power.

I rubbed my temple, wishing for a stronger painkiller, knowing full well it wouldn't make any difference. I needed to concentrate on my mission; distractions were no better for me than for the others. My eyes narrowed as I surveyed the terrain before me. The Cyborgs were out there—I could feel it—and I had no doubt they would see us before we saw them.

Soon the signal came; it was time to go. As we moved across the parking lot, Pathfinder led our group toward the west entrance of the building, while Broadside had his team fan out and head toward the loading docks. Having them spread out probably saved some lives, because that's when the Cyborgs struck.

A thin beam of energy streaked out from behind a pile of crates on the loading dock, striking Angelheart in the chest. As she went down, I heard a muffled report from behind me, and a Cyborg trooper jerked upright and fell over backward. Longshot had lived up to his name. He began laying down cover fire for the advancing Resistance fighters, with Broadside and his military cohorts strafing the loading docks with their assault rifles.

The skirmish seemed almost ethereal in the night, with the sizzle of the Cyborgs' energy weapons and the soft staccato of our weapons, all of which were equipped with sound suppression. It was far too quiet for a battlefield, yet the bodies hitting the ground were all too real.

Then I lost sight of the main battle as the loading docks passed from view. We were nearing the side entrance when I heard another sizzle and Dart screamed before a second shot silenced him permanently. Pathfinder collapsed, grasping his shoulder, his pistol clattering to the ground. Codecracker stooped down to help him just as a Cyborg rose up and drew a bead on her.

I dropped to one knee and raised my gun in a two-handed grip. The Cyborg spotted me but hesitated, a confused look in his eyes that quickly turned to resignation as I gunned him down. I saw movement a little further down the walkway and shifted my aim. These weren't Cyborgs, but the regular security guards. I dropped two of them before the remaining guard retreated.

By the time I reached Codecracker, she had Pathfinder on his feet and was urging him toward the entrance. She glanced back at me. "Nice shooting, Bonner. Thanks."

The look in that Cyborg's eyes still vivid in my mind, I simply nodded and headed to the door. I peered through the window; no guards were visible in the corridor. When the others caught up, Pathfinder kicked the door open.

Codecracker gave me a grim smile. "The security system has been offline for about ten minutes now. I told you we had it covered." She glanced back with furrowed brows at the sounds of fighting at the loading dock, then went in.

She guided us down the hall, stopping in front of the third door on the left. A couple of steps behind us, I could hear Pathfinder's harsh breathing. He clutched his left arm, the shoulder of which had a nasty laser burn. His face was pale and damp with sweat. But his eyes were alert as he watched the other end of the corridor for signs of enemy forces. I had no doubt that his good right hand would wield his gun effectively should the need arise.

I did the honors this time. Placing my shoulder against the door, I gave a good heave and popped it open. "After you."

Codecracker entered the room and crossed over to a computer terminal on the far side. Pulling up a chair, she switched it on and waited for it to boot up. When the login screen came up, she reached into the pouch at her side and pulled out an oddly shaped device which she plugged into a port on the side of the machine.

Pathfinder had taken up the lookout position at the door, so I followed Codecracker and leaned against the edge of the desk to take a little weight off my bad leg. The login screen disappeared; she was in, although I didn't see her make any keystrokes. Now she went into action, fingers dancing over the keys, eyes glued to the screen with unblinking concentration. Data streamed across the monitor; I could see her eyes following the text. Then they widened slightly and her mouth opened with a small grin. She jabbed a couple more keys, then sat back with a soft sigh. Tiny activity lights started flickering on her device.

She noticed me looking at the object and said, "It's a decryption and storage module I designed a while back. I'm on the sixth version, I think." Her tone of voice did not carry any boasting, just a simple statement of fact.

We watched the progress in silence for a moment, then she turned to me again. "By the way, thanks again for taking out that Cyborg out back there. He had me dead to rights. I owe you my life."

I decided to try a bit of levity; the trembling in her hands indicated that the shock of what almost happened out there was beginning to set in now that she wasn't focused on the computer. "Hopefully I wasn't too much of a distraction."

That elicited a quiet chuckle. "Yes, well, sorry about that. You deserve better." She looked down at her hands as if willing them to stop shaking. "I just worry about my people."

"I know," I reassured her. "It's a sign of a good leader."

"Maybe." Her expression turned dark. "I don't even know if I have a team now."

Pathfinder spoke up from the doorway. "If that were so, the Cyborgs would be here by now. Don't give up hope. With Longshot up high and Broadside on the ground, they stand a good chance. At the very least they're keeping Morgren's monstrosities busy for us."

I felt my eyebrows raise. "Morgren's monstrosities? That's a new one."

The darkness in Codecracker's face seemed to deepen. "While the Cyborgs aren't technically part of OSaR's Intelligence group, they seem to fill the hardcore enforcer roll whenever Morgren needs them. He operates in the shadows while others do his fighting. Typical Intelligence agent." Her eyes darted to me in embarrassment. "Present company excepted."

I waved it off. "There are agents who do fit that description. Some of us prefer to keep our skills up to date. Operating in the shadows brings risks of a different sort; sometimes a bit of field work is a welcome change."

"Our sources said Morgren is off-planet, working on the Mars insurrection." Codecracker grimaced. "That doesn't mean he doesn't have his tentacles extended elsewhere, of course."

She shook her head. "What gets me is that Cyborg you took out. It looked like he froze for a split second. Cyborgs don't freeze, they just kill."

I shrugged. "Maybe he was surprised that I got the drop on him. Cyborgs are only human."

"Just barely," she muttered, jaw muscles tightening. "You've surely seen the reports from the surgeons and science staff. Their cybernetic implants do more than just make them better soldiers; they inhibit their emotions, maybe even destroy their personalities. Their humanity is gone, stripped away by the Technology."

Leaning back in her chair, she exhaled loudly. "There have even been reports that some Cyborgs have resisted their implants, their emotions conflicting with their programming until they snap."

It was my turn to flex my jaw muscles as I nodded in agreement. "This is true. I've seen it firsthand. In one case, the Cyborg went berserk in a crowded city street. There were a lot of casualties, military and civilian, before he was stopped."

"It's frightening what the Order's Technology is doing to people." She stared into the monitor for a moment, her eyes not really focused on anything, then went on. "OSaR didn't even invent this Technology. They found it hidden away somewhere. They don't even know where it came from. But they are making use of bits and pieces of it as they figure it out."

She made a sweeping gesture across the computer and the module attached to it. "That's why we're here now. Pathfinder found out that this system is now connected to the main OSaR network. Hence the term 'system hot.' The Order is trying to bring all of their divergent systems in sync to enhance interoperability. But it also provides access in less secure environments like this to those who know how to crack the code."

"Like you, for example?"

She smiled, almost a bit shyly. "It's kind of an obvious nickname, I suppose."

"It fits." I bobbed my head toward the computer. "So what are we looking for here?"

"The key to the Technology."

Now my interest was truly peaked. "The key?"

She rested her elbows on the arms of the chair, steepling her fingers beneath her lower lip. "We've pulled a number of data dumps in recent years, trying to piece together information about the Technology in hopes of finding a way to neutralize it. The big brains in the Resistance have found evidence that a key exists that can control the Technology. We don't think OSaR has decrypted this information yet. It's not clear whether the key is a code, program, or physical object, but indications are that it can shut the Technology down completely."

"What do you mean, shut it down?" My conversation was sparkling by now. There was a lot of information to process, enough that the throbbing in my head was forgotten. The possibilities presented here were at once exhilarating and terrifying.

"I mean that everything would be terminated. According to the data, if the key is applied correctly, all of the Technology just stops. Weapons, starship augmentations, communications . . . everything. Even the cybernetic implants in the Cyborgs."

Things began to click in my mind. Maybe that was Director Rousseau's ace in the hole. If the Cyborgs were to rebel, he could simply shut them off. No, that didn't quite track. It sounded like this key would destroy everything, not just the Cyborgs—unless there was a way to apply it selectively. A momentary chill came over me as the full implications set in. The implants were tied directly into the Cyborgs' brains and nervous systems, basically replacing parts of the brain. If they were disabled completely, the Cyborgs would die.

My thoughts were interrupted by a double-snap from Pathfinder. He was peering through the door down the hallway. "I hear movement at the other end," he hissed. "I think our time has run out."

Codecracker slammed her fist on the desk. "No! The decryption isn't complete."

"Is the data itself downloaded to your module?" I asked.

"Yes, but the decryption routine needs to be connected to the network. It works through codes contained in the system. Without them, the data is useless." She paused, then took a deep breath, resolution settling into her features. "There is another place I can finish this."

She quickly typed in a code and the lights on the decryption module went out. With a slight pop, she disconnected it from the computer and returned it to her pouch. "Let's get out here," she said, sliding out of her chair and heading for the door.

We nearly made it to the exit before the double doors at the other end of the hallway slammed open and a dozen security guards burst through. Pathfinder and I unleashed a volley of gunfire in their direction, scoring a few hits and causing the others to duck for cover. That gave us the time we needed to get outside as the guards began returning our fire with a blistering hail of bullets.

I heard Pathfinder gasp as we cleared the doorway. Glancing back I saw him limping, blood quickly soaking the leg of his trousers. I almost missed the fact that Codecracker had turned north when we got outside; I was expecting to head southwest to where we had left the trucks.

"This way," she called, picking up speed.

Knowing that Pathfinder would never be able to keep up, I slid to a stop, intending to give him a hand. I needn't have bothered. He had stopped behind a steel drum on the walkway. He waved me off and crouched down, bracing his gunhand on the top of the drum. The door we had just exited from swung inward, disgorging the pursuing guardsmen. Pathfinder opened fire, nailing a couple of them and driving the rest back through the doorway.

I turned and sprinted off to catch up with Codecracker. She was waiting around the corner of the building, her little pistol in hand. She shifted the barrel away when she saw me.

"Where's Pathfinder?" she said, trying to catch her breath.

"He's not coming," I answered, the sound of gunfire accentuating my words. "He's got them bottled up for the moment, but it won't last."

Uncertainty distorted her features, but dissolved as she nodded, eyes downward. She knew as well as I that he was giving us time to escape and complete our mission. And that he did not expect to escape himself.

She spun around and headed out the north gate at a quick trot. Crossing the street, we turned right up another alley, then sidled through a gap in the fence around another warehouse. This lot was deserted; the warehouse was not in use and no security was present. Making our way across the lot, we exited through another gate and made for a groundcar about twenty yards down the street.

Swinging around to the driver's side, Codecracker motioned me to get in the other side. She fired up the ignition and we took off with a screech of rubber on the pavement. The car sped toward the city, slowing down to normal speeds as we reached more populated territory.

It was a quiet ride for a few minutes. Finally, Codecracker spoke. "We have a handful of backup vehicles scattered around the target site, just in case."

"Good thinking." It didn't surprise me at this point. This team had demonstrated efficiency and intelligence in their planning and implementation for as long as I had been with them. No wonder they had enjoyed so much success. Until now. The Cyborgs had tipped the balance, but they still held their own while we broke into the OSaR network. I would be curious to find out if any of the Resistance fighters survived, though not entirely surprised if they did.

We appeared to be moving across town. I ran through potential destinations, but nothing important lay in this direction. "Where are we going?"

"To my apartment," she responded.

Now that was unexpected. "Aren't you afraid of blowing your cover?" I asked. A vital part of the security for the group was to remain anonymous to anyone outside their cell, including Command and Intelligence agents like me, with the exception of their primary contacts. What we didn't know, we couldn't tell.

She shook her head. “It’s not important anymore. The only way to finish decrypting this data is to access the OSaR network again.” She scowled at the road ahead. “Once that’s done, I’ll send it off to my contact and then try to get off-world. I’m compromised now. My usefulness here is over.”

We rode in silence a bit farther. Codecracker fidgeted, her expression and posture radiating the anxiety boiling below the surface. Finally, she apparently decided to distract herself with small-talk.

“Tell me about yourself, Bonner. You handled yourself pretty well back there.”

“I spent eight years in the Earth Defense Force Marine Corps. You learn a little something about combat in the Marines.” I smiled. “Perhaps a little more than your typical Intelligence agent.”

She grimaced. “I already apologized. You’re not going to let me live that down, are you?” We turned onto another street and headed west. “So, were you still in the EDF when OSaR staged its coup?”

“No. By that point I had married and resigned my commission. Jill and I wanted children and I decided to get a job where I could come home at night and my family wouldn’t have to worry about whether I was still alive or not. When the Order took over, I toyed with the idea of joining what was left of the EDF in the Resistance, but we decided it would be best for our son if we just stayed neutral.”

I grimaced. “Thinking I could stay out of it was my big mistake. One day, about five years ago, OSaR came for me.” My fists clenched at the memory. “Four Cyborgs entered our apartment, demanding that I come with them. I resisted."

As I told my story, it seemed so long ago, a life long forgotten. Yet I forced myself to remember, to relate the experience that I had never shared with anyone before. "I killed one of them, but it wasn't enough. By the time they were finished with me, I was a broken, bloody mess."

"Unarmed?" Codecracker asked incredulously. At my nodded affirmation, she said, "Why aren't you in prison, or dead, for that matter? Any soldier who could take out a Cyborg like that would be considered too dangerous to let go."

I rubbed the thigh of my gimp leg, eyes shut tight against the pain lancing through my skull—and ripping through my heart. "By the time I got out of the hospital, they no longer considered me a threat." I took a shuddering breath. "I don't know what they did with my wife and son. I've never seen them again."

I felt the warm touch of her hand on mine.

"I am so sorry," she said softly, the sincerity in her voice almost as painful to me as the memories.

It had been years since I let myself recall that part of my life. I felt drained, my emotions warring with the need to fulfill my duty. Slowly, the ghosts of my past faded as my mind refocused on the task at hand. We weren't finished yet.

The groundcar slowed as Codecracker turned into the entrance of the parking garage of a tall apartment building. She managed to find a spot not too far from the elevators.

Her apartment was on the seventh floor. She punched in the key code and we went in. It was a nice suite, with a contemporary air about it. She motioned to the living area. "Make yourself at home. I'll be out in a minute," she said as she disappeared into the bedroom.

I decided to forgo the plush couch in favor of one of chairs at the dinette table. I surveyed the room, noting a variety of knick-knacks and mementos, until a picture on an end table caught my eye. It was a photo of Codecracker and a young, dark-haired man. They looked happy and in love. Nothing else in the apartment bespoke of a male occupant.

The bedroom door opened and Codecracker gave me a wave. "Be there in a second," she said, then stepped back in and strode over to the bed. Her appearance was changed. Not only had she cleaned up, she was now wearing a red blouse, black skirt, and red heels, with matching jewelry. She picked up a little box from the pillow, then reached over to the dresser and grabbed a makeup case.

As she came back into the living area, I pointed to the picture. "Nice looking couple. Your husband?"

Her pace slowed a bit, then she came over to the table and sat down. She opened the makeup case and started arranging items on the table. Finally she spoke.

"We were almost engaged," she answered, eyes misting as she picked up the little box and opened it. Still holding the box, she looked up at the picture. "Trent was kind of shy, but he was getting ready to pop the question. We had a date scheduled one night; I knew what was coming. His sister was terrible at keeping secrets. He never showed up."

"What happened?"

"OSaR happened," she bit out savagely. She set the box back down and rubbed her hands together, agitated. "Trent had just completed his Master's degree in Cybernetics and Robotics. OSaR tabbed him as a potential risk and had him picked up." Her eyes came up to meet mine. "I learned later that Morgren himself made the risk assessment and ordered his arrest."

She shook her head. "Trent had no interest in either OSaR or the Resistance; neither did I. Like you, we just wanted to live our lives. He . . . we . . . never had a chance. Trent didn't survive the interrogation."

"I'm sorry." It sounded lame, but I couldn't think of anything else to say. At that moment, I meant it. This conflict had caused so many people so much pain. It needed to end. Maybe tonight's efforts would be a catalyst to help bring it closer to a resolution. The irony of the situation struck me. OSaR—and Morgren—had detained and killed an innocent man on the possibility he might be an insurgent, leading the woman across from me to actually join the Resistance and become a major thorn in their side.

She sniffed and wiped her eyes. "Thank you, Agent Bonner."

I inclined my head in acknowledgement. There didn't seem much else to say. I gestured toward her box. "Okay, you've piqued my interest, Codecracker."

"Not Codecracker; I'm done with that. It's Sandra. Sandra Cahill." She offered me her hand. "Glad to meet you, Agent Bonner. Do you have a first name, or do I make one up?"

I grasped her hand. "Adam," I said, with some hesitance. It had been some years since anyone called me by my first name.

"Adam," she repeated. "It fits. As to what I'm doing," she looped an elastic band around her head, using it to position a magnifying lens over her right eye. "I'm sure an intrepid Intelligence agent can figure it out. Eventually."

Lifting the box again, she reached for a pair of fine-tipped tweezers and carefully removed a tiny, flat object from inside the box. She carefully set the object on the back of her left hand, then placed a small strip of something over it. The strip looked like the type of synthetic flesh you might find in a med-kit. Next, she began to apply makeup to the strip, to blend it into the skin of her hand. When she was finished, it looked like a small scar.

"An identity chip." My eyes widened. "You're an employee of OSaR!"

"Very good." She gave me an impish smile. "I knew you could do it." In a more serious tone, she explained, "I'm a computer tech with OSaR. It provides a good cover and knowledge of their systems. While I can't dig around sensitive databases at work, I have been able to learn enough to crack their network from other locations, like we did tonight."

She held up her left hand. "My identity chip was never implanted. The doctor who was to perform the procedure is sympathetic to the Resistance. He provided me with a supply of synthetic flesh to help me fake the implant."

The audacity of the plan and her success in carrying it out impressed me still further. "You remove it and leave it on your bed when you are engaged in your nocturnal activities."

"Right. It fools OSaR's GPS into thinking I'm at home, all tucked in like a good girl."

"And now you're going to use the identity chip to gain access to the office—and the OSaR network." This was a dangerous game she was playing, but having realized the significance of the data she collected, I understood her logic. She was going to decrypt the data and then disappear.

She nodded. "Right again, Adam. I'm going to have to work fast to finish the decryption and get out of there before Security catches on."

Pushing her chair back from the table, she stood up and let her gaze wander about the apartment. I knew she did not plan to return. Whatever the outcome of tonight's incursion, she would not be back. Most likely, she had contacts in the Resistance to help her get passage off Earth. Getting out of the OSaR building and reaching those contacts was going to be the real trick.

She turned to me. "You don't have to come. I'll be all right."

I shook my head adamantly. "No, I'm coming. I have to see my mission through, too." There's no way I was going to let her out of my sight now. I would see this through to its conclusion.

The journey to the main OSaR building wasn't long. We approached a side entrance and Codecracker held her hand up to the sensor. With a click, the door opened. She led me down a hallway to the staircase, avoiding the security desk nearer to the elevators. She seemed apprehensive, almost as if she expected alarms to go off at any moment. Her security clearance was fairly high; apparently that was enough not to send up any flags to the system when her ID chip was used.

We climbed the stairs to the third floor. She waved at another sensor and the door opened. The lights were dimmed in the corridor at this time of night, but they were more than enough to illumine our way down the hall.

Codecracker stopped in front of her office door. She inhaled deeply. "This is it," she said, activating the sensor and pushing the door open. She stepped into the room and froze.

"Good evening, Sandra," Director Rousseau's voice came from inside. "Please, come in."

Codecracker glanced back at me as she walked toward the Director. I followed her in, taking in the scene before me. Director Rousseau stood near a desk on the left side of the room, one of his scientist's, an older man named Kempf, beside him. To the right were two security officers, with a third just inside the door. All three guards had their guns drawn and trained on us.

"Director Rousseau, this is a surprise," Codecracker responded. She gestured toward the desk. "I left some files here I intended to take home this weekend."

Rousseau's dark eyes narrowed. "Now, now, Sandra. No need to keep up this pretense," he said, motioning to one of the guards.

The guard approached Codecracker and relieved her of her purse, handing it to the Director. Rousseau looked inside. "What is this?" he asked, lifting her decryption module up.

"It's a decryption and storage device, Director," I responded before she could say anything.

She spun toward me, mouth open, with an expression both hurt and betrayed.

"Well done, Mr. Morgren!" Rousseau said, peering at the device intently.

Codecracker's face went from hurt to utterly horrified. For a moment, I felt the impulse to draw my gun and take out the guards, but it subsided quickly. The Resistance cell was broken, its leader captured, and vital information gained with regard to how such cells functioned. Plus the added bonus of information and decryption algorithms contained on Codecracker's device. My mission was complete.

The Director eyed me for a second. He may have noticed my moment of discomfort. Then he said, "You may go now, Mr. Morgren. Head down for debriefing, then pick up your next assignment."

Without looking at Codecracker, I spun on my heel and left the room. The door clicked shut. I paused a little ways down the hall, muffled voices sounding in the room behind me. I couldn't make out the words, but Rousseau's poisonous voice sparred with Codecracker's defiant one.

Then I heard a single gunshot and I knew Codecracker . . . Sandra . . . was dead. Even as the tears welled up in my eyes, the emotion behind them melted away as my programming kicked in. My headache intensified as the cybernetic implant in my brain pushed my feelings into the dark abyss of forgetfulness.

As I stood there, I fought against the ache to remember, to recall my wife and son. Their images drifted in the fog at the edge of my memory. Their faces remained shadowed, the touch of their love fleeting at the fringe of my heart, but unable to take hold.

Slowly, the pain faded and my thoughts returned to the present. I headed for the elevator. I would be debriefed and receive my next assignment. There would always be a next assignment. Though we had disrupted one cell, the Resistance still lived. The Order entrusted me with finding and breaking them. I was very good at my job.

As the elevator doors began to close, in the back of my mind I wondered if the Resistance would ever find their key and shut down the Technology. Completely.

Then maybe the pain would end.

God Spot

C. K. Deatherage

Red gaseous clouds swirled outside the Captain's cabin windows, obscuring the glistening stars that lay beyond the nebula's particle-dense formation. Janet Langston sat at her desk, chair turned facing the viewport, eyes transfixed, unseeing, on the roiling clouds. Her gaze did not take in the reflection of the mid-fifties woman, with graying blonde hair and slate gray eyes, dressed smartly in her form-fitting Navy blue uniform. Her nose did not detect the irritating odor of leaking lubricant wafting from the ventilation shafts. Her ears were deaf to the groaning and creaking of her wounded ship. For the moment, her senses had shut down, her mind too tired to process more discouraging data. Then the door chirped, startling her back to awareness. She swivelled her chair around and cleared her throat. "Enter."

Commander Sullivan's tall frame passed through the doors. "I have the ship's current status report," he said, setting a computab in front of her.

She took it reluctantly. "Any good news?"

He thought for a moment, running his long fingers through his close-cropped red hair. "Engineering has traced the fluctuations in the Environmental grid. They should have everything locked down soon."

"Wonderful," Janet could hear the sarcasm in her own voice. "That leaves only the damage to the tachyon drive, the auxiliary systems, the hull breaches on decks 13 and 14, and the wreckage in craft hangar three to repair—not to mention eight injured crew members."

"No one was killed," her First Officer pointed out.

"No, not in this attack—but what about the next?" She leaned back in her chair, rubbing her temples tiredly. "It's been two weeks since the Cha'potl began attacking us, refusing to answer our hails. They haven't even asked us to surrender the ship—it seems their intent is to blow us out of their sector in tiny pieces."

The Commander nodded, his blue eyes concerned. "I know it seems an impossible situation—"

Janet interrupted, gesturing sharply, her voice harsh. "It *is* an impossible situation. Security beacons and patrol posts ring this sector too thickly to bypass. Security webs are scattered at random within the bounds of Cha'potl space, and the wormhole through which we blundered into this misplaced corner of hell is unstable and erratic on this end. All avenues of escape are cut off. We can only hide in this nebula so long—the Cha'potl have all the time and resources they need to track us down. We are caught, and the rope is slowly tightening around our necks."

"Ensign Duvall and Lieutenant K'a'Vish are working to see if there is a pattern to the wormhole's behavior," Sullivan responded hopefully. "We may eventually be able to calculate its next location—"

"*May* isn't good enough, Sean. We must find a way back through that wormhole—or our deep-space assignment ends here, permanently."

"We'll make it." Janet looked up at her First Officer. His face was calm, sure, a rock of stability in her storm-tossed world. He continued speaking. "I have every confidence in your abilities and that of the crew. We'll get through—but," he gave a crooked smile, "a little prayer couldn't hurt."

"Prayer?" she snorted, "That's your department." She fingered the computab he had delivered. "You remind me of Tim the Theologian."

"Who is he?"

"Someone I knew as a first-year cadet. His real name was Timothy R. Schmidt."

"Tell me about him."

Janet knew what her First Officer was trying to do: take her mind off her discouragement, redirect her thoughts to a more peaceful period in her life—a common stress-reduction technique taught by the Deep-space First Contact Academy. Very well, she'd play along. She closed her eyes, resting her head against the back of her chair. "Tim was studying to be a science officer along with the rest of my class. We called him the Theologian because of his insistence that all sentient beings possessed a belief in a supreme Creator—whether they admitted it or not. He called it . . . a God-spot, an inner longing to connect with someone higher than ourselves."

She sat forward, picked up her mug of lukewarm coffee and took a sip, grimacing at its tepid temperature. "He received a lot of ribbing from us, but he could give it back. He called us his Agnostic Angels."

"Sounds like a regular character."

She nodded. "He was. I missed our lunch-time debates when he was called home due to a family emergency—though once when I thought his remarks were too personal, I—well, I responded rather rudely." She took a second sip. "He took it well, though. Few things fazed him. I heard he later finished his studies and took a science post on the Deep-space Exploration Vessel *Starling*."

"I'd like to meet him someday," Sullivan said, then grinned. "It would be fun to hear what you were like during your Academy days."

Janet's lips twitched in answer to his amusement. "I was just as stubborn and temperamental as I am now—only with youthful inexperience to exacerbate the problem and no First Officer to calm me down."

Sullivan's grin broadened. "Did it work?"

She picked up the computab and pretended to study its data. "Aren't you supposed to be on the bridge?" she queried.

"Aye, Captain."

She watched him leave, the doors swooshing shut behind him. He was a good First Officer—and someday he would make a good captain. She sighed, turning back to her desktop viewer where she had been analyzing her entries before drifting off. The first record was for two weeks ago.

Captain's Entry. Ship Time: 52387.9

An extraordinary day by all accounts. We've made two startling discoveries in one work shift: the salvage of, according to Lt. K'a'Vish, a 200-year-old Saatu escape pod, which, more importantly, was drifting near the entrance of the wormhole an Avarti merchant claimed was in this sector. The wormhole is a beautiful anomaly, much like that near Quadrant Two, but smaller in scale. We've sent a long-range probe through the wormhole to test its stability and direction. So far, the readings appear positive. We will continue to study the anomaly before deciding whether to chance traversing its corridor. Meanwhile, Lt. K'a'Vish and Chief Engineer Casella are thoroughly examining the Saatu vessel for useful components. Even 200-year-old Saatu technology holds advancements beyond ours.

Captain's Entry. Ship Time: 52507.5

The long-range probe has picked up fluctuations at the far end of the wormhole, which could indicate some instability. However, readings thus far still point to a reliable passage, and unless further readings prove otherwise, the consensus is that we attempt it. As for the Saatu vessel, Chief Engineer Casella has in effect labeled it "space junk." While it appears to have a prototype of a transhyperian drive with energy cells still intact, its age and small size would prohibit its use in the Columbus' *tachyon system. I suggested she try modifying the drive to fit a minicraft, a possibility which she reluctantly agreed to investigate. Unfortunately, the vessel's data modules were too corrupted by age to download, and as Lt. K'a'Vish is unaware of any significant Saatu encounters in this region, we may never know how the pod reached its ancient resting place.*

She paused her analysis. The Saatu escape pod. Something clicked in the back of her mind. What if two-hundred years ago the Saatu tried to invade this sector through the wormhole and somehow the Cha'potl drove them back? A failed invasion would explain the Cha'potl preoccupation with security, closing the borders of their space, and viewing the unstable wormhole and those who enter through it as a threat to be neutralized at all costs. No exceptions, no attempt at communications—just destroy the threat. She exhaled a long breath. Her ship and crew could be caught in a 200-year-old war. Her mind churned. Was there any way to test this theory? Someway to convince the Cha'potl they were not in league with their ancient enemy? Maybe the Saatu pod could offer more insight into her theory—that is, if it had escaped the bombardment that had left craft hangar three a smoking ruin.

She heard the comm chirp as Sullivan's voice interrupted her thoughts. "Captain, we're being hailed."

Her mouth went dry. "The Cha'potl?"

"No." Her body sagged in relief. Surprised, she noticed her hands were trembling—too much lukewarm coffee and not enough sleep. Sullivan's voice continued. "It appears to be a scrambled message on a low-range subspace frequency. I . . . think you want to hear it for yourself."

"I'm on my way."

As the doors separating her cabin from the bridge slid shut behind her, she nodded towards Ensign Duvall. "On screen." She kept one eye on the viewscreen while making her way to her command chair. The viewscreen flickered and a fuzzy image of a brown, leathery face appeared. The lower half of the creature's visage was distorted, leaving only his yellow eyes glinting clearly at the captain.

The Commander commented, "The signal is coming from a small beacon our scanners picked up about forty kilometers off our port bow." He nodded to Ensign Duvall at Operations. "Replay the message."

"Aye, sir."

"Can we adjust the visual?" Janet asked, squinting at the blurred image.

"I'm afraid not, mon Capitaine," Duvall replied, his response tinged with a hint of his native French. "The distortion appears to be purposeful."

The audio crackled then settled into gravelly tones. "This message is for Captain Janet Langston of the Commonwealth Deep-space Exploration Vessel *Columbus*. I have information that is vital to your survival. If you are receiving this, please respond." The visual flickered, and the message repeated itself.

Janet studied the distorted features carefully. If this alien had found them, tucked away inside the swirling dust particles of the nebula, what was to prevent the Cha'potl from spotting them as well? They were running out of time.

She drew a deep breath, exhaling slowly, feeling the eyes of the bridge crew on her. "Let's hear what this message has to offer. Open hailing."

"Captain, I must point out this could be a trap," Lt. Commander Rigel's British tones cautioned from behind Tactical.

"I am aware of that possibility, Commander. Open hailing."

"Aye, Captain."

She raised her chin, summoning her full authority. "This is Captain Langston of the Commonwealth Deep-space Exploration Vessel *Columbus*. I have received your hail."

Immediately, the image on the viewscreen became animated, the creature's yellow eyes glowing with anticipation. "Captain, how fortuitous my scanning beacon located you! Your features and voiceprint had been broadcast on all Cha' potl channels. One moment as my program confirms your identity." The image flickered; then the alien's distorted visage reappeared. "Identity confirmed. This is indeed a pleasure. Allow me to introduce myself. My name is unimportant. Suffice it to say, I belong to a race known as the Somona, and I am a student of the stars. I have spent a lifetime studying this sector and as much of the galaxy as my scanners would permit me to view. However, I yearn not only to view the galaxy from afar, but to explore it, engage new cultures, expand my horizons and my life. Thus, I have spent the past thirteen years studying the wormhole through which you entered this sector. It is the only way in or out—as the Cha'potl, our self-proclaimed guardians, have effectively closed off all contact with the outside, imprisoning us in the name of safety and prosperity. But let me come to the point as time is of the essence in this venture."

The yellow eyes appeared to lean forward conspiratorially. Janet wished she could see the creature's entire face. It was disconcerting to listen only to a pair of eyes set deep in a tanned forehead. The gravel-voice continued, "I know the secrets of the wormhole, Captain. I can calculate when and where it will appear and for how long it will remain open—and I am willing to give this information to you, provided you give me information on what lies beyond the wormhole: star charts, cultural records, species' encounters—anything that will aid me once I make my escape."

The eyes retreated as the form leaned back. "If you are agreeable, we will need to meet to exchange information. My beacon will download the coordinates to your computer. You will need a small vessel to traverse the security web within this region, and you must—*must*—stay within the flight parameters I transmit or you will trigger a security breach. If you are willing, we must meet within the next twenty-one hours—or it will be too late. I do not believe you will survive until the next opening. You may be my last chance for a new life—and I yours. I will await your arrival at the coordinates noted—and may the heavens smile upon you." The eyes lowered as the visage bowed.

"I'm receiving the coordinates, Captain," Duvall acknowledged; then he gave a startled exclamation. "The beacon just self-destructed!"

From the helm, Ensign Rüder snorted, muttering in German.

Janet turned towards him. "What was that, Mr. Rüder?"

He looked over his shoulder, ice blue eyes setting off his short white-blonde hair. "Nothing, ma'am. I just said it is an impossible mission."

"Impossible," she murmured, turning the message over in her mind. If the Somona's offer were genuine, their situation had just changed from the impossible to the miraculous. She turned to Sullivan. "Assemble the chief officers in the Planning Room."

* * * *

All were silent around the table. Janet could feel the tension in the room.

"So." Sullivan said. She turned towards her First Officer. He continued, "You are going to meet with this unnamed Somona."

"That's right."

He sighed. "Captain, I don't like this set up. It smells of a trap."

She shrugged. "We won't know unless we try. And if he were working for the Cha'potl, why didn't he just give them our coordinates once his beacon located us? Why arrange for a rendezvous?"

"Perhaps the Cha'potl want to separate you from your ship, to force information from you that would aid them in overpowering *Columbus's* defenses," Lt. Commander Rigel pointed out. He rubbed his neatly-trimmed brown moustache with one finger—a gesture Janet knew reflected his unease. Then he tugged at the silver insignia at his wrist, another sign of worry from the reserved English officer.

Janet felt a small shiver slide down her neck. Meeting with the Somona was a definite risk. "That is why if I don't return in nineteen hours I want you to move the *Columbus*," she answered. "I don't want to know the new location—what I don't know, I can't be forced to tell."

Silence. Marguerita Casella, long black hair bound in a tight ponytail, stared furiously at some invisible spot on the table. Heinrich Rüder looked down at the computab he was fingering. Dr. Wentworth Billingsly scowled and drummed his thick fingers against the table with unnecessary vigor, an angry glint in his green eyes. Only K'a'Vish, Martin Duvall, and Sean Sullivan maintained eye contact with her, and Martin looked horrified. Janet forced a cheerful note into her voice. "Come now, we mustn't assume the worst. Let's review the scenario. Martin—"

Ensign Duvall blinked and keyed in the command sequence to project the image of the Somona's coordinates onto the Planning Room's viewscreen. "The rendezvous point is .009 light years from our current location," he said. "Traveling in a Type 6 minicraft at maximum drive—"

"Why a Type 6?" Ensign Rüder queried.

Casella answered. "It's the only one that's still intact. The others all suffered some damage when the hangars were hit."

Duvall continued, "—it would take the captain 8.47 hours to reach the coordinates, which appears to be an uninhabited M-class planet. The surface and lower atmosphere suffer from frequent electromagnetic storms, making it difficult for patrol ships to scan for lifeforms—which is probably why our Somona friend chose the location."

"The electromagnetic storms would also prohibit the use of communications," Rigel said. "You would have to land the minicraft on the planet's surface with no transmissions."

Janet nodded. "I had planned on it. Furthermore, there is to be no attempt to send subspace transmissions to and from the minicraft in transit—we can't risk the Cha'potl intercepting and tracking the messages."

Again there was silence. Janet wished the scenario were more hopeful, that they could pull out of their circumstances without depending on the unknown Somona and his calculations. She felt a twinge of nerves, a tingling foreboding. With the survival of her ship in the balance, her crew depending upon her, she felt suddenly—small. She swallowed. This was no time for personal insecurities.

"Captain, if I may suggest, you should not go alone. An additional member would increase the chances of success if something should go wrong." Lt. Commander Rigel paused, tugged on his dark blue officer's jacket, then added, "I volunteer to accompany you on this mission."

Janet smiled at her old friend, whom she had known since Academy days. Norman, of course, would volunteer—and he was right. Two members on this mission would double its chances of success. Before she could respond, Ensign Rüder spoke up.

"Actually, with the trick flying required by this course, I should be the one to go."

Several other voices began to speak, but Janet raised her hand. A warmth replaced the cold nerves she had been fighting. Her officers, her friends, each willing to join her on this dangerous mission, each willing to sacrifice him- or herself for the ship, for their captain. She studied the faces turned in her direction, drinking in their earnest expressions. "I thank you for your offers, but—" she hesitated. "Heinrich, I need your skills at *Columbus*' helm. Doctor, you must remain here as well. Norman—"

She longed for Rigel's comforting, logical presence, but if anything should go wrong, she needed his expertise to remain on the *Columbus*. They would need him to get home—provided they could escape Cha'potl space in one piece.

"Captaine," Duvall's voice broke in, "I should be the one to accompany you as I would be in the best position to evaluate the calculations and coordinates the Somona gives us."

Martin Duvall had already been working on a way to forecast the wormhole's behavior and was a logical choice. Yet, she felt a reluctance to accept his offer. He held a special place in her heart—she had watched him mature in his role, developing into a competent and assured officer, and she wanted him to make it home. If the Somona proved to be working for the Cha'potl, if they should trigger the security web in transit, any number of catastrophic ifs would mean neither she nor Martin would see home again. Then again, if this mission were not successful, none of the crew might make it home. She fixed Duvall with a probing gaze. "Are you sure, Martin?"

His head raised, brown eyes snapping, pride at being chosen evident in his bearing. "Oui, mon Capitaine."

She nodded. "Very well, Ensign, you're with me. We leave within the hour."

* * * *

Janet tugged her blue jacket closer to her throat, the wind sending her hair whipping in several directions at once. To her view, the vista was nothing but rust red desert, splattered with clusters of dusty green bushes and broken by jagged lava outcroppings—perfect for an isolated rendezvous but not a place she would want to visit for shore leave. The wind had a pungent bite to it, tingling her tender sinuses. She glanced down at the scanner clutched in her right hand: one lifeform reading eleven meters north, crouched behind a rocky tumble of lava cones.

"He hasn't moved for the past three minutes," Ensign Duvall informed.

"Maybe he's the shy type," she answered, trying to ease the tension they both felt. The twin scanners chirped, and Duvall muttered, "He's moving now at a fast clip. Eight. . . now six meters away."

They both looked up. A shadowy form hunkered down behind a copse of bushes, a metallic glint blinking between the waving branches.

"Weapons?" Janet asked, studying her own scanner.

"Negative, Captain—at least, not any that register in my readings."

A crusty voice called out. "I don't recall saying you could bring company!"

Janet raised her head and shouted back. "I don't recall your message forbidding it either!"

A strangled wheezing issued from the bushes, which Janet interpreted as laughter. "An oversight on my part." The lifeform stood and began trotting towards them. As he drew nearer, Janet saw he wore a brown cloak, covering dusty brown trousers and boots. A hood shadowed most of his features, and one end of the cloak was thrown over his lower face, leaving only pale yellow orbs glittering from the hood's interior. Apparently, she would see even less of the Somona's face in person than she had in the video image.

"Captain." The Somona bowed. "I trust you have brought the needed information for this exchange?"

"I have." Janet held out an opened canister containing twenty-three computabs. "These records contain star charts and cultural information on species we've encountered in our journey through several quadrants. I trust you will find them useful."

The Somona reached out a leathery hand and touched the canister. "A treasure indeed," he rasped reverently. He paused a moment longer, then reached inside his robe. Janet heard Duvall slide his blaster from his belt as a precaution. The Somona opened his hand to reveal a small metallic cube that glistened in the morning sun. "There," he breathed, "there lies a lifetime of study—and your salvation. This datacube contains the location for the next wormhole appearance, which, my dear Captain, will occur a little less than seventeen hours from now."

Janet caught her breath. "That doesn't leave us much time."

The Somona shook his hooded head. "I have no control over the wormhole, Captain. I can only give you its coordinates—the rest is up to you."

The wind picked up, flinging fistfuls of red sand at the trio. "Captain! My scanner is detecting an electromagnetic storm heading this way!" Duvall called above the rising bluster.

The Somona strained his vision into the wind. "You must leave quickly, Captain. These storms are unpredictable: they could last for a few hours—or a few days. You have neither to spare."

"I agree." Janet handed the datacube to Duvall. "Let's go." She paused a moment, turning back to their unnamed ally. "Thank you." Simple words, but she meant them with all of her being. The Somona bowed and raised one hand. "May the heavens smile upon you," his gravelly voice intoned; then, clasping the canister of computabs close to his body, he turned on one booted heel and scampered agilely back across the blowing desert, the wind and sand erasing his footprints.

Janet blinked, eyes tearing in a vain attempting to wash out the particles bombarding her vision. She coughed, holding one hand before her nose and mouth. "We've got what we came for—let's get out of here."

"Aye, mon Capitaine," came Duvall's muffled agreement.

She began jogging back towards a ridge of lava outcroppings behind which rested the minicraft, Duvall keeping pace several meters to her left. Gusts of dust-filled currents ran their gritty fingers through her hair and uniform, making her long for a heavy Somona cloak to absorb some of the sand-blasting her skin was receiving. It was difficult to see much more than a few meters ahead as the ground began to climb, changing from whirling sand to porous lava rock. Peering at her scanner to make sure she was still heading in the right direction, she stepped carefully past jagged edges of broken stone and around the grasping branches of hardy bushes. As she glanced to her left to check on Duvall's progress, she heard a muffled snap. Her right foot broke through a thin crust of porous rock, flinging her body forward. Landing with a sharp grunt, she felt the rough surface of the lava rock scrape the first few layers of skin from her right cheek, and drive its many teeth into her outstretched palms. Her scanner clattered down the side of the outcropping, lost in the swirling sandstorm.

"Captain?" Duvall called out, moving towards her.

"I'm alright," Janet called back, silently berating herself for not watching her step. "I just—"

A deep groan issued from the ground beneath her, followed by a sharp crack. "Stay back!" she shouted. She stopped trying to extricate her foot from the hole that encircled her ankle and lay still. For a moment, the rock around her seemed to stabilize, and she released the breath she'd been holding. Then, with a crackling roar, the earth disintegrated.

* * * *

One by one her senses began to return. First was sound—a low, steady moan. Janet concentrated on it. The wind, echoing within a chamber—a tunnel. Another part of her mind supplied further information: a lava tunnel, the roof collapsed. More sound. Pebbles dropping, bouncing, clattering against stone; sand shifting, sliding against rock. A voice, calling. The odor of dust next assaulted her nose. Taste followed on the heels of smell—the pasty flavor of dirt mingled with blood. She tried to spit out the offensive mixture but coughed instead. That awakened her tactile sense with a vengeance. Pain—everywhere. Her own moan mingled with the wind's throaty lament.

Gradually the blur of agony segmented itself into localized injuries. Leg, left leg broken—she recognized the symptoms immediately, having broken her leg in a Scrambler race as a teenager. She forced her mind to analyze her body's signals. It hurt to breathe deeply—possibly bruised or broken ribs, again on her left. Tentatively, she tried moving her head, gasped, and quickly thought better of it. A sharp pain radiated from her left shoulder to her breast bone—more broken pieces. Rough rocks wedged themselves uncomfortably in the small of her back. Her right ankle throbbed. A sticky wetness oozed across her forehead and down her left cheek. This was not good. She swallowed, grimacing at the taste of blood and sand. On the other hand, she was still alive, and as she hurt all over, it meant that her spinal column was still intact.

"Captain!" The voice was louder, clearer now. She opened her eyes, felt a moment of panic as her vision focused on empty darkness. She blinked, allowing her sight to adjust to the dim features of the tunnel. Overhead was a large, gaping hole—maybe 15 meters above. Swirling purple clouds edged with lightening filled its circumference. Further down from the hole, against the far wall bobbed a light—Duvall's wrist beam. Martin! Janet forced her mind to alertness. In the light from the aperture, she could better judge her situation. She was on her back, buried by debris. Only her right arm and shoulder and head was exposed. A large flat slab lay slanted atop the rubble constraining her, crushing against her left side, pinning her against the rough floor of the tunnel.

The light bobbed closer. Janet could see Martin's shadowed form dashing across the rock-strewn floor towards where she lay. "Captain!" He skittered to a stop beside her, collapsing to his knees. In the glow of his wrist beam, she could see his dark hair matted with sweat against his forehead, dirt streaking his face, smudging his uniform. His large brown eyes locked onto hers. He swallowed, shoulders going limp. "You're alive," he whispered with relief.

"For now." Her voice sounded rough with dust and pain.

He flicked his light across the tossed rubble. Janet could see his mind racing, trying to plan how to extricate and move her to the minicraft—a hopeless task. She steeled herself for what she had to say.

"Martin." He looked at her. She licked her bruised lips, tasting blood. It hurt to draw enough wind to talk. She took shallow breaths. "You've got to get back . . . to the *Columbus* . . . plot a course to the wormhole . . . use the coordinates in the Somona's datacube."

He shook his head. "Not until I get you out of here."

"Martin," she put more urgency in her voice, "there's no time. You've got to lift off . . . before the storm grows stronger."

He began to pull some of the loose rocks away from her body. "I've piloted in worse," he answered.

Janet felt frustration and panic mounting in her. She forced her voice to remain level. "There's not enough time. You have little more than . . . nine hours to return to *Columbus* . . . before they move the ship. You've got to leave . . . now!"

His features were set in determined lines as he hefted another rock into the darkness. Janet closed her eyes, summoning her inner reserves. "Martin." Her voice was clear, sure, the voice of a captain. He stopped his efforts and looked at her. She could see the stubbornness—and fear—in his eyes. "Rigel was right . . . to suggest a second member for the away team . . . in case something went wrong. You are that second member. It's up to you . . . to see that this mission doesn't fail."

His gaze faltered, the stubbornness wilting. His dark eyes pleaded with her. "I can't just leave you."

"Yes—you can." Janet locked her gaze on him, her voice taking on a harsh authority. "That's an order, Ensign."

He stood slowly. She didn't take her eyes off of his, willing her own strength and resolve into him. He swallowed, then nodded. "Aye, Captain."

Relief left Janet feeling shaky, but she maintained her firm gaze. Duvall hesitated for a moment longer, then turned and slowly began to pick his way across the tunnel floor. Before he passed from the light into the shadows, Janet called one last time. "Martin!" He turned. She drew a deep breath, ignoring the sharp pain in her chest. "Get them home!"

"I will, mon Capitaine," came his reply. Her eyes traced the bobbing of his light as it began to climb slowly toward the ragged hole far above. Stones slithered and dropped at his passage. She strained to catch the outline of his form as he pulled himself upright out of the opening. He paused, appearing to gaze down into the tunnel. She doubted he could actually see her, but she drank in that last blurry image as he turned and disappeared from view.

She closed her eyes, sighing—and waited. The wind increased its moaning, and in the distance thunder and the sharp crack of lightening split the sky. Even down in the tunnel Janet could smell the acrid odor of singed molecules and feel the tingle of electrical forces unleashed. She listened for the roar of the minicraft's engines, but could hear nothing over the wind and storm. Eternities passed in minutes, and minutes slowly trickled away. Surely, Duvall had lifted off by now: he was gone. She swallowed, noting a growing thirst. Then she breathed deeply—she was alone. An odd coldness coursed through her, and she shivered. Enough of that, she snapped at herself. It was time to get her mind onto other things, time to do something, time to take control. She might have sentenced herself to die, but it would be on her terms—the Langstons never took death lying down.

She studied her surroundings in the purple light of the storm. She could see that the slab lying atop the rocks pinning her down rested partly against a ledge jutting to her right. If that ledge supported some of the slab's weight, then she might be able to dig her way from beneath the rubble. With only one arm free and functional, that would take awhile. Tentatively, she stretched out her right hand and grasped a rock wedged near her chest. Her fingers dug into its pumice-rough surface. She hefted and threw it in one motion. Bone grated, muscles tore—and Janet cried out. Gasping, she lay still, tears of pain trailing down her temples, muddying the dust in her hair. Gradually, the searing jolts faded to a steady throb. Nausea welled up, and she swallowed painfully, willing it to subside. Well, that isn't going to work, she silently admitted. Her body was too battered to dig herself out. Here was where she would remain until death overtook her. She tried to reconcile herself to that fact, wondering how long it would take.

She forced her mind off of herself and her hurting body, focusing on the last image she had of Ensign Duvall. "Poor Martin," she whispered, recalling the desperate look in his eyes. He would probably bear the guilt of leaving her for the rest of his life—despite the fact he had only followed her orders, that there had been no choice in the matter. Yet, he would labor under the haunting refrain, "Could I have done something different?" She knew—she had sung that refrain too often herself. Images of crewmen who had died under her command flittered through her mind: faces, names, comrades, friends. She drew a shuddering breath, remembering the wrenching pain she experienced every time a member of her crew died, always pondering, "Could I have done something different?" Well, now the life-or-death situation was her own—and she had made her decision when she ordered Duvall to leave.

A cool breeze brushed her face, filled with the musty odor of darkness. It seemed to permeate her body, wrapping its cold breath around her spirit. Gasping, Janet felt her heart pounding, her hands beginning to tingle. She couldn't get enough air. Inhaling deeply, she winced at the pain it caused, her fear increasing with each pang. Sweat beaded on her forehead, mixing with the blood and stinging her lacerated skin. A flash of anger coursed through her. Get a hold of yourself, Janet Langston, she thought. Panic is unbecoming in a Commonwealth officer. She forced herself to breathe evenly, and her fear subsided. That's better. She had to focus her mind on things other than death—that would come soon enough. She tried to picture her ship, her crew, her officers, to feel their presence, to sense their thoughts. Marguerita in shirtsleeves, half buried beneath an Engineering console, spanners spread on the floor, Spanish curses punctuating her repair efforts. Heinrich, arrogant, vulnerable Heinrich Rüder, brilliant blue eyes shining as he executed near impossible maneuvers at the helm of the *Columbus*. K'a'Vish, her black hair contrasting with her pale blue skin, yellow eyes both gentle and curious, a walking repository of Sabaetian knowledge. Sullivan, his Irish-blue eyes dancing with laughter or shining with an inner strength, an earnest concern for his crew, for his captain, faithful to speak his mind yet mindful of the wounds his words sometimes inflicted. Norman, dear loyal friend and counselor, so calm in his British demeanor, yet possessing a depth of emotion that he seemed unaware of. But Janet knew—she'd seen it in his eyes, in the quirk of his brow, a twitch of his lips, the subtle pride with which he spoke of his family. Martin, eager, sensitive Martin. One by one she summoned images of her crew, past and present, of good times and bad, of laughter shared publicly with friends and tears too often shed in the privacy of her quarters. And she thought of her ship. *Columbus*. . . .

* * * *

Her ear tickled. Janet jerked awake, breathing heavily. She was drenched in sweat. A tiny rivulet running into her ear had stirred her back to consciousness. She felt as if she were roasting—her throat was parched, lips cracked. She blinked against the bright sun that burst into the cool darkness of the tunnel, heating up the ground, the rocks—and her. The storm had passed, and the sun was directly overhead. It had been early morning when she and Martin had met with the Somona; now it was noon, or close to it. Duvall should be halfway to *Columbus* by now, maybe more. She tried chewing on her tongue to stimulate her salivary glands. It worked—a little. She shifted, trying to put her face in the shadow, but stopped, groaning at a sharp stab from her broken shoulder. Death wouldn't be so bad if only it didn't hurt so much getting there.

Death. Her throat tightened, as that all too familiar coldness brushed its fingers against her mind. Death was there, lurking, waiting for her to quit fighting. Why was she struggling to stay alive? There would be no last minute rescue, no miraculous recovery. The *Columbus* could not pass through the security web to fetch her; the minicraft was too slow, the Commonwealth too far way. Even the Cha'potl didn't know to look for her here. But the fact was, she didn't want to die—not here, not now, not like this—trapped, pinned helpless in a black pit, hidden on some godforsaken world in the middle of a Cha'potl-run hell. So far from home, from friends, family. Alone. A sob escaped her cracked lips.

She fought to control her emotions. Commonwealth officers weren't supposed to indulge in pity parties, especially captains. They were to stride bravely to their deaths, face the enemy's fire without flinching, go down with the ship, be mourned and honored by their crew, have their names inscribed on a Commonwealth memorial plaque. Only she wasn't ready to trade life for a spot on a plaque. She would gladly go down with the ship—if she could see it one more time. Bring on the enemy. Anything but this slow, crushing weight, this isolation. That was the worst part—to die alone, helpless.

She swallowed against the lump in her throat and willed the inner coldness back to its hiding place. It retreated—reluctantly, whispering of its return. For a long time she lay still, thinking of nothing and everything:

Fizziwig, her orange tabby, alternately cuddling up and purring or else pouncing on her feet in bed when she was home on leave; John—a sharp pang there—waiting so long, so patiently, yet finally, finding another with whom to share his life; Admiral Brighton, who had seen her leadership potential and had convinced her to switch to a command track; Cadet Schmidt, Tim the Theologian, whose spirited debates had enlivened many a noon meal.

So many things Janet regretted, words said and unsaid, things left undone. She sighed, opening her eyes. The heat was less intense now—in fact, she could feel the coolness return to the ground, chilling her sweat-soaked uniform. The sun had long passed its zenith; it would soon be setting, signaling the close of day—and the close of her life. She knew she would not survive the cold of night. She watched as the finger of sunlight crept across the floor and up the wall behind her, its dust-flaked ray taking on the red of sunset. She tried thinking of something else. Martin should have reached the *Columbus* by now—they might even be on their way to freedom, back through the wormhole, back to life. It would be worth it, if her crew could escape, could continue on their exploratory trek, and then home.

As if hearing a silent cue, the inner coldness began creeping back into her mind, her body. The *Columbus*, gone . . . that would leave her truly alone—alone with the darkness growing. A dark, grasping cloud roiled around her mind, her soul, eclipsing the feeble comfort her memories had given her. Soon, even the light would abandon her to her death. It was too much. The black horror clutched at her throat, heaved within her chest, and burst forth in a ragged cry. "O God!" she sobbed, "God, no!"

She wept, surrendering to the tears at last, and from somewhere deep within a desperate longing fought its way to the surface, groping, until a single plea found its way to her lips. “God—please . . . ” she whispered, gazing at the distant, fading light. Gradually, her sobs slowed to shuddering gasps, then to calm, even breathing. The horror faded; the cold gave way to a numbing warmth. Her body relaxed, lungs drawing shallow breaths. From the back of her mind came a warning, but she no longer listened—it no longer mattered. The sky visible through the hole above was a deep purple edged with rose red. Already a smattering of stars had begun to glitter in the upper reaches. She watched as the red faded, more stars joining their comrades. Out there, somewhere among those glistening gems was the *Columbus*—going home. Janet closed her eyes. It was enough.

* * * *

Thrumming, a steady pulsating thrum, like the warming heartbeat of a mother surrounding an enwombed babe. It was a comfortable, familiar sound. There were other familiar things too—smells of air scrubbed clean of dust and irritants, electrical smells and antiseptic. A voice calling—again familiar. Janet opened her eyes, blinking into the sun high overhead. No, it wasn’t the sun—a light. All at once her disassociated senses coalesced. *Columbus!*

“Janet?”

She was lying on her back on a medtable, various lights blinking around her, probes and transmitters sending data back to the medical console. Her First Officer was leaning over her to her left, the doctor to her right.

"It might take a few moments for the stimulant to work," Billingsly informed. "She's been sedated for three days, remember."

Janet found her voice. "*Columbus*." She swallowed; it was difficult to talk. She felt very weak and her tongue didn't want to work properly.

Sullivan smiled. "Captain—welcome back. You've had a rough ride." He squeezed her right hand gently. Her left arm and the lower half of her body were immobilized and numb.

The doctor snorted. "A ton of rock applied to the human anatomy tends to leave very little intact. However," he paused, filling another injector and applying it to her neck, "I've managed to do a bit better than all the king's horses and all the king's men at putting you back together again—though it's taken the better part of three days to do so. You won't be playing in the gymnasium soon, but you'll be back risking your life in no time, I'm sure."

It was so good to hear the doctor's stinging Bostonian accent. The injector seemed to free her tongue a bit more. "The wormhole—are we through?"

Sullivan nodded. "The last leg was a dash to the coordinates with three Cha'potl cruisers on our tail—but it was there, just where the Somona said it would be. We're now on our way back to the Avarti outpost to make repairs."

She looked down at Sullivan's large hand, still holding hers, then back up. "How did I get here? There . . . wasn't time."

"The transhyperian drive from the Saatu pod—you told Casella and K'a'Vish to adapt it to a minicraft, remember? Well, they managed to salvage it from the wreckage in the hangar, and K'a'Vish and Duvall went back for you. The old drive gave out just shy of the wormhole, but they made it through before we did. We caught up and brought you to Medical."

"Where, I might add," Billingsly interrupted, "I have had a terrible time keeping the crew from flooding Medical with get-well gifts. I made Duvall take them to your quarters."

A smile tugged at Janet's lips and she closed her eyes. She was still very tired, but a contented tired.

"I think our patient needs to rest," the doctor intoned, removing Sullivan's clasp.

Janet opened her eyes once more. "Sean . . . ."

He paused, looking down at her.

"Tell Martin, K'a'Vish—everyone—thank you for me."

He nodded. "I'll do that. Anything else . . .?"

"One more thing." She paused. "When we get back home . . . remind me to look up a certain science officer."

"Tim the Theologian?"

She nodded, letting her eyelids shut out Medical's lights, sinking back into the comforting thrum of the ship. Her lips framed her final thoughts before she drifted off to sleep. "I owe him an apology."

Little Bit

S. L. Rudder

Colton Stafford glanced over at his seat-mate and rolled his eyes. He then leaned closer and softly spoke into her ear, "You know, you might need that some day."

Marie stopped gazing out the viewport beside her and turned to her husband with a huge grin. He had caught her once again attempting to chew the tip of her finger off in her nervous excitement.

"Well, I guess you will just have to hold my hand for the next hundred light-years or so to keep me from doing it," came her standard reply.

Grasping her hand, and lifting it to his lips for a gentle kiss her husband looked lovingly into her eyes and replied, "THAT will NOT be a problem, Babe."

With pure contentment, Marie snuggled up against her husband's shoulder. She returned to gazing at the expanse of space outside the viewport and let her mind drift back, thinking about how they had gotten to the place they were now.

Two years earlier, when both were only twenty-one, Marie Dillard, a linguistic/cultural specialist, and Colton Stafford, a data retrieval/technology expert, had been first year Science interns on the crew of Desmond Elias Silverman. They had been on Captain Silverman's deep-space vessel when first contact was made with the Vlivlarians. The young couple had been thrilled to work along side, even in very minor roles, the Captain and his ambassador wife, Constance, as relations and later a treaty were set up with these advanced beings. That was how Earth became the newest member of the Vlivlarian Space League of Worlds. Long, hard hours spent working together on all of this led to much stronger feelings than just friendship, and six months ago Marie and Colton had been married.

Now, they had the honor of being part of the survey crew on the first ever joint venture between Earth and the Vlivlarians. In fact, they were two of only eight people from Earth to be included. It was a remarkable honor, hence Marie's excitement and anxiety.

A few months past, a Vlivlarian cruiser had discovered a previously undetected Draknaroki outpost on a routine flight from the Vlivlarian home word to Earth. To their dismay, the entire installation had been completely devastated. The only clue they found passing by was a message beacon that was broadcasting on all wavelengths and a wide variety of both known and unknown languages the same message over and over.

That message was simple: "Threaten us, you die."

The origin of this beacon was unknown and, for their own security, the Space League had decided this called for much further investigation. The Science division saw this also as a wonderful opportunity to learn more about the little known race from Draknaroke Prime and its surrounding system. Colton and Marie agreed whole-heartedly with this assessment.

The Draknaroki were a little known and very war-like people, and operated under a code of high honor. Their definition of what that meant was not always clear to those races dealing with them. They attacked with little provocation anyone who dared wander into their part of the universe or that broke their code. Their warships were highly advanced and extremely well armed making an encounter with them potentially very deadly. The Vlivlarians had made more or less friendly contact with them in the past and had set up a very limited and tentative agreement with the race. About the only thing known of them at this point, beyond their war-like tendencies and a smattering of their language, was their physical description.

The Draknaroki were a solid framed, humanoid race who tended to be slightly taller and more muscular than people from Earth. Their skin tone had a slight lavender to purplish hue, with their hair normally a darker shade of their skin's coloring, hair color generally leaning more toward the blue side of the spectrum with skin more toward the red. Both males and females most often wore their hair long and flowing or pulled back into intricate braids. They were an extremely strong and athletic people, well in keeping with their physical build. Warriors of both genders preferred hand-to-hand or melee weapons for ground combat as opposed to pistols or beam weapons, although they were experts in the use of these as well. Their facial features were strong and chiseled, not unattractive, and very similar to Earth humans. The main exception was the ridges that ran from their noses, curving out across their cheek bones, and flowing back to their hairline just above their ears. These ridges could be anywhere from a single one on each side, to groups of as many as four, and differed greatly in width, depth, and protrusion. Perhaps their most unsettling characteristic was their eyes which were cat-like in pupils, shape, and coloring. Their teeth were more pointed than Earth humans and also had a slightly more feline appearance, though without the extended fangs.

Even with their tentative agreement, no Vlivlarian, or any of their allies, had ever set foot on a Draknaroki planet or base. The opportunity to survey and study this destroyed outpost was one that could not be passed up, and to be chosen as two of the Earth's specialists was indeed a great honor for the young couple.

Colton retrieved his techpad from his carrypack and pulled up the information they had been given at the mission briefings. Marie leaned close to read along with him, even though they both knew the facts practically by heart, having gone over them so many times. The speculation, mainly based on the discovered recording, was that the outpost was a secret military base. This was generally accepted, although there were no records of the Draknaroki ever placing this type of installation so far from their home system. The reason for its existence was unclear, but the working theory was that it was an arms and weaponry R and D facility. Because of this belief and the fact that they still had no idea where the warning message originated from, the scientific team and ship was not alone on this mission. They were accompanied by four heavy warships carrying multiple armed strike teams to guard the researchers on the ground and squads of fighters for added protection in the air.

A high pitched bell tone signaled that they had reached their objective, and the small fleet came out of hyperspace over the planetoid outpost. Colton leaned across his wife, craning his neck to see if he could catch a glimpse of their destination from the small viewport beside her. This time it was Marie's turn to smile over his excitement.

There was little to see other than a rocky planetoid that looked very similar in appearance to the Earth's moon. The only differences being its coloring, which was a light teal, and that sparse areas of vegetation could be noted in certain areas. Before landing, the science vessel would send out orbital probes to take readings of the entire planetoid and its atmosphere. Air quality should not be a problem since the Draknaroki had much the same requirements as humans from Earth. The Vlivlarians might need breath masks to compensate, but Colton and Marie, along with the rest of the Earth's crewers, should be able to breathe on their own.

A second pair of bell tones rang out, followed by the announcement that all personnel could leave their seats, move about the ship, and begin gathering their gear, if need be, in preparation for landing.

Colton rolled his eyes once again and chuckled as Marie squealed and jerked his arm so hard it was as if she were trying to dislocate his elbow. The couple left their seats with the rest of the passengers, but they actually had little to do to get ready. The larger part of their equipment was in the hold and would have to be unloaded after landing. Their techpads they kept in their carry-packs as well as their handheld techscan units. They had packed their clothing module as soon as they woke that morning, and it was ready to go when they were allowed to disembark.

The pair made their way, along with many others, to the observation lounge where they could watch the readouts that came in from the probes on the large tech-screens. Both were ready to make note of anything they might need to watch for when they made landfall.

The reports streaming by were brief and to the point. No lifeforms. No standing structures. No land-to-air weapons. No working tech of any kind. No dangerous radiation levels.

"I hope there is something to look at down there," Marie said as she scanned down the next report, this one listing the lack of harmful gases, plants, or wildlife.

"I am sure we can find something," Colton reassured her. "Just because there are no standing structures or working tech doesn't mean that we won't be able to get something up and running. We should at least be able to get a good idea how they used the structures from the debris found in the area."

"I know, but I was hoping for a lot more." Marie took a seat on a nearby sofa. "I have learned as much of the Draknaroki language as we have on record, which was enough to set up a translation program that will hopefully fill in the gaps. I have also read every bit of information I could find on the Draknaroki people. There isn't much out there, but what little I found is fascinating!

"If we could figure out more about Draknaroke Prime, and the Draknaroki Honor Code, I think we could make great steps toward getting them to join the Space League. I would much rather have them as full-fledged allies than to have to worry about going to war with them some day. You've seen the read-outs on their warships!"

Her husband joined her on the couch, once again reaching for the finger that was on its way toward her lips. "I totally agree. We do need to face the idea that, if this is a R and D outpost, they may well be gearing up for war. There is no way to know until we get down there and take a look."

Yet another bell tone alarm sounded with the announcement that all probe data had been received and analyzed. This was followed by another signal and instructions for all passengers to return to their jumpseats and fasten their restraints in preparation for landing.

Not caring about appearances, the young couple raced back to their seats. Their behavior drew annoyed looks from some, and knowing smiles from others on the team. Most of the Vlivlarians seemed simply to be mystified by yet another form of strange human behavior.

Touchdown was actually quite smooth, but the Vlivlarians believed in taking all precautions in all situations. This was a fact that sometimes caused the people from Earth a few headaches, but they were learning to adjust. Taking chances to obtain information, or for any other purpose, was not something their Vlivlarian hosts could understand. The idea of nothing ventured, nothing gained was a concept beyond their comprehension.

When the all clear bell sounded, Marie and Colton eagerly found their places in line, and tried to wait patiently for their turn to leave the transport, Colton holding both of Marie's hands to save her poor fingers. There had been so many meetings both before the trip and in route, that all knew what was expected of them. There was no need for further discussion or to wait for orders upon landing.

As they cleared the exit ramp and reached a place where they could finally get a look at the outpost, the pair stopped dead in their tracks in shock. Neither of them were even able to speak at first. Reading reports and scans was one thing, seeing it all with their own eyes was something else. The scene before them was complete and utter devastation. Not only were there no standing buildings, there was not even an upright partial wall within their line of sight. Huge pits gaped where the outlines of structures could still be seen. What little plant life there was in the area was scorched and burnt for almost a kilometer around the outpost's perimeter.

Colton shook his head in disbelief. "Doesn't look like I have much hope of finding any tech to work with in this mess."

Marie placed her hand on his arm, "Don't give up so quickly. There may be a little bit left. Some areas could be in better shape. We did just get here after all."

"I know, glass half full, right?"

"At least half full." She gave him a brilliant smile.

The first course of action was teams making general scanning sweeps with hover crafts, working in a grid pattern across the ruins of the outpost. Their findings were added to the data from the space probes. Much of the destruction was complete, but there were areas that had not been entirely razed to the ground. The preliminary scans reported nothing that could be identified as weapons emplacements or spacecraft debris. There was also nothing that could determine what the purpose of the base had been. The discouraged researchers spent the evenings comparing findings and entering data. The Staffords began to feel as if they were making the same entries each day. Nothing of interest found.

"Even if this was an R and D outpost, I can think of no reason that would call for such hateful destruction," Marie murmured to Colton one evening as she lay on his shoulder before they went to sleep for the night.

"If we knew *who* had taken out the outpost, it might be a little bit easier, but not much," came the sleepy answer from her husband, followed by a very large and lengthy yawn.

Even with only being married for six months, Marie knew the signs. If she did not roll off his shoulder now, very soon he would snore her off. She reached up and gave him a soft kiss on the cheek.

"Good night, my love. Tomorrow we get to do our own exploring on the ground. Get some sleep."

The only answer she received was a small snort showing that her husband was already out for the night.

Bright and early the next morning, the young couple was up and ready to start the day. The previous evening, using the hover craft scans, the research crew leaders had mapped and divided out into plots the entire outpost area for small two- and three-person teams to go over more throughly on the ground. The exception to this procedure was the five-person team who drew the kilometer-wide burn zone on the perimeter. They, along with the support of a full strike team, would make their way clockwise around the entire area. Not that any of the search teams held out much hope of finding anything.

The Staffords were once again going over the readouts of the scans, both from the orbital probes and the hover crafts, on their techpads as they walked to their designated area.

"You know what is really weird, Colt?" Marie asked as she ran a portion of the list back to the top for a third time through.

"You mean besides me?" Colton returned with a smirk.

Marie poked him with an elbow. "Yes, besides you. I am getting pretty used to your weirdness." She held the techpad over for him to see. "These readings, right here in this section. There are very few Draknaroki remains reported anywhere. But in our designated area, there are none."

"Yeah, I noticed that. Do you have any guess why?"

"None whatsoever. I was hoping you might have a brilliant deduction to share."

Colton gave her a cheeky grin. "Six whole months of marriage, and I still have you fooled into thinking I'm brilliant."

Marie gave him a small, half smile, "I'm serious, Colt. Doesn't it seem strange that if this was an R and D facility, there would be a whole section with no remains of troops or workers of any kind?"

"Maybe they had enough warning that they all gathered in safer areas or something. Not that ANY areas were safe from what we have seen so far."

"I know, but our area is the ONLY one with NO remains. With all the other mysteries around this place, I really want to take our time and figure out why."

Having reached the edge of their zone, the couple stopped. They stared out across the rubble and burned empty space not only of their area, but the entire base. The thought of all the lost lives, knowledge, and resources brought looks of regret to both of their faces. Colton turned to face his wife, his arm going around her waist for a quick hug.

"Okay, Babe, I'm with you. After all, if we are going to do this job we are going to do it right. Besides, the Vlivlarian captain has scheduled an entire week for the ground level scans. We have plenty of time to use."

Marie threw her arms around his neck, nearly cutting off his wind. "I knew I could count on you," she whispered in his ear.

In accordance with the Vlivlarians love of continuity and symmetry, each team was to work in the same search pattern. They were to scan in swaths, the first pass north and the return one south, starting at the southwest corner of their individual plots. All data was input for comparison on the shipboard techscreen system with the findings then available for download on individual techpads. Each evening, Marie and Colton joined the other teams in the lounge where findings were compared and discussed.

The teams found little of interest for most of the first two days. Very few Draknaroki remains had been discovered, a much smaller number than expected for an outpost of this size. And with the exception of a few handheld weapons, no real defensive weaponry or even components had been located at all. Nothing more than the outline of buildings were found in most places. Some of these were quite large, but there was nothing to hint towards their purpose left to be seen.

The first hopeful find came late on the second day when the teams with the bottom and top plots on the extreme west of the scan zone each discovered similar structures that had somehow escaped being totally demolished. Early on day three, the teams with the top and bottom plots on the extreme east found similar structures. Much study would be needed to determine the functions of these finds, but they were the most promising things any of the teams had come up with to that point. The searchers were slightly encouraged that there might be a chance of possibly finding some useable data hidden away.

The Staffords had drawn the exact center section of the search area. After the finds of the last two days, they hoped to make a discovery of their own. Late the following morning that hope was realized. Continuing to make their scanning passes, nearing what should be the center point of the outpost, they found a fifth partial structure. This one was in better condition than any of the four previous ones—if you could call having sections of slightly less than a meter high walls being in good condition. The most exciting part was that the interior floor was a good three meters lower than the surrounding ground level, and partially intact. Furnishings of some kind could be seen in the rubble near the broken walls.

The young couple called in, reporting their find and requesting their larger equipment be sent out to their location. Sharing excited smiles, they proceeded to do an in-depth investigation of the ruin.

Techscans set at their highest levels, Colton and Marie carefully went over every centimeter of the outline of the building and the partial wall before proceeding inside. Two thirds of the floor was gone, exposing a basement level below. On the remaining third they could just make out what looked to be computer control banks. With a gleeful cry, the young data/tech vaulted the wall and rushed over for a closer look.

"Watch out for that floor!" called his wife. "I am NOT ready to become a widow after only six months!"

She might as well have saved her breath. Colton was so intent on his techscan that he did not even hear her.

When Colton reached his destination safely, with only one foot breaking through the floor at the edge of the hole, Marie was able to let out the breath she had been holding. Shaking her head, she followed him with much more caution, and peered over his shoulder to see the readings on his screen.

"Look here, Babe," he said as he noticed her presence behind him. "This section right here looks like a data storage area, and it is nearly intact. If I can restore it and run it through the linguistics program you came up with, maybe we will have our first clue as to what this outpost was here for."

Marie's eyes swept across the control panel to the right of the section her husband was studying. "Colt, I'm pretty sure this writing here says 'base protection shield, main unit control'. It looks like we've found the central hub for some kind of force field generator."

Colton brought out his techpad and keyed in the words she had pointed out to him. “You’re right, Marie. That’s what it says. As much as you have been studying the language I shouldn’t be surprised though.”

Marie’s face flushed with pleasure at the look of pride from her husband. It was really nice to be appreciated, especially by the man she loved.

“See if you can make out any more of these labels while I work on this data system.”

After making notations of all the labels still readable, Marie left her husband’s side to do a little bit of exploring on her own. As she approached the edge of the hole in the floor, she saw a stairway on the far side of the structure that had not been visible from the outside.

“I’m going to see if I can get down there, Colt.”

Colton waved a hand over his shoulder at her, “Yeah, Babe, whatever. Wait! What?” He turned to give her his full attention. “Just you be careful. I like having you around too.”

With a shake of her head, she gingerly made her way along the edge of the outside wall until she was even with where the stairway should be. Carefully, she worked her way over the broken section and jumped down on to the stairs, testing each step as she went.

As was to be expected, the area under the collapsed portion of the floor was buried deep in rubble, and a hand-held techscan would not be able to penetrate it. Anything that might be found over there would call for some digging. She would have to report the find and wait until more excavation equipment could be brought to the location to do any searching in that area.

Pulling her own techscan out of her carrypack, Marie began working her way around the part of the basement she could walk in. Not really knowing what to look for, she used a high level, wide spectrum scan, giving the device little attention as she let her eyes roam over the debris while it did its work.

Above her, she could hear her husband's direction to the support techs who had evidently arrived with their heavy equipment. She went on exploring, knowing that he would be occupied until he had things up and running, if that were possible. His mumbles and grumbles as he set up made their way down to her as he began working.

Marie's eyes were drawn back to the techscan when it gave a small beep noting a discovery of some sort. To her surprise, the readout showed the outline of a possible door in the corner farthest from the stairway. She proceeded toward it, keying in a search for a latch or locking mechanisms. Brushing her hands through the dust on the wall, she was able to make out what she believed to be the outline of the door. The crack was so minute it would have gone unnoticed if she had not known of its existence. It followed the edges of the masonry that formed the walls of the basement and had no straight or hard lines.

She was still tracing this, when her techscan finally picked up a possible latch. Looking at the indicated location to the right of the door, all that could be seen was a continuation of the masonry wall with just the slightest indentation, which could easily be taken for flaking off of the surface.

Marie paused, her thumb hovering over the likely spot. She wondered if she should report this find and wait for instructions, or at least call Colton down there with her before attempting to open the door. Overhead, she could still hear him grumbling at his equipment.

"Better let him be," she thought. "Sounds like he has his own troubles. I'll call in a report if I find anything more exciting."

Before she could delay any more, she pressed her thumb into the depression. Nothing happened. She tried once more, this time holding her thumb firmly against the spot. As the heat of her thumb transferred to the indentation, it began to glow slightly. With a click, the door sank quietly back and slid to the left side behind the wall. A faint light began to glow in the exposed room.

"Colt?" she called softly. "I think I found something."

"Yeah, yeah, Babe. What do you need? I'm kinda busy right now," came the distracted answer from overhead.

At just that moment, the techscan in Marie's hand beeped a warning alarm, drawing her eyes to it. It was registering a lifeform! Very faint, but unmistakable.

"Colt! Come down here! I've definitely found something!"

The urgency in his wife's voice caused Colton to forget about the program he had finally gotten to start running, and he hurried down to find her.

Marie simply placed her finger on the read-out and turned the techscan toward him as she kept her eyes focused on the only object in the tiny room: a small metal box near the back of the little, closet-like chamber. The controls on the side of it began to pulse, and display readings changed as she watched.

Colton snatched the techscan from her unresisting hand, and began checking settings as his wife moved slowly toward the box that the lifesigns appeared to be emanating from.

"This just isn't possible! None of the prelim scans came up with ANY lifesign readings!" he said as he once more checked the settings. Then he realized what his wife was doing. "Marie, stop! If this thing is right, there could be something or someone alive in there." He stepped forward, trying to grab her arm and pull her back, but missing.

Marie stood gazing down into the box through the viewport on the top, her eyes filled with wonder. Slowly, she turned back toward her husband, her eyes shining.

"It's a baby!" she breathed. "A tiny, precious, Draknaroki infant!"

"It can't be!" Colton moved closer to take his own look. "Why didn't any of the preliminary scans pick this up?" His fingers flew as he ran diagnostics and checked all the findings again.

Marie knelt down beside the box and examined the readouts and displays.

"I think this is a stasis unit." She pulled her techpad out of her carry pack and keyed to the limited Draknaroki dictionary it contained. "Yes!" she said excitedly. "I was right! It is a stasis unit! It seems it was activated when I opened the door to this hidden room."

As she spoke, a soft alarm tone sounded, and the top of the chamber slid open. The tiny infant inside began to squirm and move its hands.

Marie started to reach for the baby, and Colton caught her arm.

"Babe, do you think that is safe?" he asked cautiously. "We don't know but what this could be a trap of some kind."

"I seriously doubt that. From my studies, I found that Draknaroki cherish their children. I don't think they would use a baby as bait for a trap."

"Okay, but still. At least run some medical scans. Make sure it isn't infected with anything that might be bad for us." His eyes pleaded with her. "I don't want you to take any unnecessary chance, alright?"

Marie softened when she saw the love in her husband's gaze. "Fine, I'll run some scans, but they will have to be quick. I am dying to hold that baby!"

Colton gave her arm a squeeze. "That's all I ask." He handed the techscan back to her.

Marie carefully keyed in the proper scan parameters and held the device down closer to the open top of the unit. After what seemed like hours to her, but was actually only a few minutes, the med scans came back clear.

"See, nothing to fear," she said as she handed the device back to her husband. She reached for the baby, who was starting to show signs of regaining full alertness. Before lifting it, she did a quick check, counting fingers and toes and such.

Colton peeked over her shoulder. "Hey, it's a girl!"

His wife gave him a saucy smirk. "Right on the first try. Who says data/techs are dumb?"

"Nice! I'll have you know that even us data/techs have that one figured a long time before we reach my age." He gave her a wink and a pat on the backside. "Or hadn't you noticed that, my dear."

"Please, Colt, not in front of the baby." Marie replied in feigned shock. Then reached up and gave him a quick kiss before going on with her examination.

The baby's skin was a very soft, light lavender edging toward the pink side. The ridges on her tiny cheeks were not well defined at this early age, but there appeared to be three rows of them. Marie made a mental note to see if she could find any information about what the number of ridges might mean, whether it was a family genetic trait or if it were more random than that.

The infant's hair was a much darker shade than the young researcher had expected from the limited data she had read on the Draknaroki. It was also extremely curly, and, while coarser than a human baby's would be, it was still soft and silky to the touch. The yellow "cat's eyes" were somewhat startling at first, but they were gazing up at Marie so solemnly that their shape and appearance did not bother her too much after just a few seconds.

"She is a sweet little thing," Colton stated as he looked down at the infant in his wife's arms and gently stroked her cheek.

The baby immediately turned towards him as he spoke. Her little brows drawn down in a quizzical expression.

"I'm not sure she knows what to make of you," Marie giggled, causing the baby to give her the same look.

"You either, so it seems," Colton replied with a grin. "You keep oohing and aahing over her. I'll send a report back to base on the find, then I'm going to take a look at this contraption she was in."

"Colt, don't tell them about the baby," Marie murmured, pleadingly.

"Babe, I have to report the baby." He placed his arm gently around her shoulders. "You know we have to report this."

"I know," his wife answered with resignation. "But, just not yet. Couldn't we just wait a little while? Give her a chance to get used to us before meeting a whole bunch of strangers?"

"Alright, Babe. I will not report any of this until I finish looking around down here. Then I can make one full report instead of a couple prelims. Will that work?"

"Thanks, Colt. You're the best. You do know that I love you, right?"

"That's what keeps me going, Babe," he answered with a soft kiss to her brow.

Colton picked up Marie's techscan from where she had placed it after taking the medical readings on the baby and proceeded to examine the stasis unit in detail, starting with the outside displays.

"It would be nice if she came with an instruction book," Marie spoke up from behind him. "I don't even know what to feed a Draknaroki baby. I mean, would human formula work, or would we need something else?"

"Got no idea," came the quick answer. "Guess they will have to work that out when we get her back to the Vlivarians onboard ship." He looked around as a soft sigh sounded behind him.

"Marie? What are you thinking?"

"Nothing. I just thought that maybe, since we were the ones to find her and all, that we would get to keep her."

"Somehow I don't think 'finders/keepers' works when it comes to alien infants, Babe. Even ones found all alone in destroyed military outposts."

"That's another thing. Why on earth would anyone, war-like alien or not, bring a baby to a military outpost? It just makes no sense to me, Colt."

"That's because you are not a war-like alien. To them it may have made perfect sense."

Marie rolled her eyes at him. "Data/techs! Dumb as a post after all."

"Thanks!"

Just then, a loud signal tone went off on Colton's equipment on the level above. He dropped Marie's tech-scan unit and hurried up the stairs, much faster than caution would have called for, to see what results he had gotten for his trouble.

Marie simply shook her head, and reached over to retrieve the techscan. The unit teetered on the edge of the stasis chamber, and slid down inside before she could catch it with just one hand.

"Not too good at the one-handed stuff I guess, little bit. Maybe that will come with practice." She smiled down at the baby. "Let's just hope I get the chance to find out, shall we?"

As Marie reached down to pick up her techscan, her eyes were drawn to a lump that was showing under the lower edge of the blanket in the chamber that she had not noticed before. Curious, she pulled the blanket out, revealing a small hand-held device that appeared very similar to her own techpad.

"Wonder what else is hidden in here, little one?"

Placing the device, along with her techscan, into her carrypack, she searched the inside cavity of the stasis chamber with care. Nothing else was to be found inside, so she proceeded to make her own inspection of the outside of the box. This was not easy, as the Draknaroki infant had decided to be less puzzled and more upset at this point, and began to fuss.

"There, there, little bit. It's alright." She held the baby cuddled up on her shoulder and against her cheek, bouncing her gently. The infant quieted down, but still looked like a thundercloud about to burst when Marie chanced a peek at her face.

Continuing the bouncing, with a sway or two thrown in here and there for good measure, Marie went over every inch of the chamber. At the foot, about half way down, just below where the bottom of the interior bed was located, she found what looked like a latching mechanism. Mentally crossing her fingers for luck, she gently slid it to the side, stepping back quickly as far away as the small room allowed. With a slight pop of release, a drawer slid out of the unit, its dimensions as big as the entire base of the chamber. Inside was a large carrying case of some kind.

At this point, having noticed that Marie had not followed him back to the upper level, Colton returned to check on her.

"Stop!" he shouted as he saw her reaching for the box.

Marie jumped, and the baby cried, causing her to turn on her husband.

"What is the matter with you? You nearly scared us half to death!"

Colton slowly shook his head as he pulled her back away from the open drawer and farther from any potential danger it might hide.

"You can't just open drawers and grab the contents of some alien hardware, Babe. Come on, you're smarter than that. I thought it was us data/techs who were dumb."

Marie gave him a rueful smile as she jostled the baby, trying to calm her down again.

"I just didn't think. I'm sorry, Colt." She motioned with her head, pointing her chin towards her carrypack. "I found what looks like a data device of some kind hidden in the baby's bed. You might want to take a look at that. I just wanted to know what was in this drawer I found when I pushed that latch."

Colton gave his bride a long-suffering look, which quickly broke into a smile when she raised up on tip-toe to give him a kiss on the cheek.

"All forgiven?" she asked with her best big-eyed, innocent look firmly in place.

"For now, but I may require further payment in the not so distant future." He returned her kiss and added a cheeky grin. Taking in his wife's rosy cheeks, he said, "You two match up pretty well color-wise, don't you."

"Colton James Stafford!" she replied in mock fury. "You just behave yourself! You hear?"

Colton just grinned, and started going over the stasis chamber on his own, taking readings and feeding them into his techapad.

"Did you learn anything interesting up above?" Marie asked remembering the beeping sound that had called him away.

Still gazing at displays and dials, he replied, "Not yet, just a 'done downloading' signal. Your translation program is working on it now."

Satisfied with the readings he had obtained both on the unit and the drawer's contents, Colton carefully lifted the box out of its hiding place. Making one more quick pass with the techscan, he opened the lid. Inside was what appeared to be baby clothes and supplies. "Looks like someone believed in being prepared," he said holding up a little outfit for his wife's inspection.

Marie moved closer to get a better look. "Let's get this up top where there's more light so we can see what's in there."

The couple carefully climbed back up the stairs, Marie carrying the baby and her carrypack, and Colton bringing the large hidden box and all its contents.

As they reached the small expanse of solid flooring, Marie turned to her husband.

"Colt, you better go ahead and report the stasis room down there, along with the baby."

"You sure, Babe?"

"Yes," came the firm reply. "I just realized there could be more of those hidden chambers. What if there are more stasis units with survivors? We need to get them out and cared for as soon as possible."

She gave the baby a gentle hug. "Maybe you can just ask if we can keep her here for now and bring her back when we come?"

"I'll see what I can do. But no promises."

"I know, Colt. Just try."

Colton went to work on the data device they found with the baby, plugging it in to the translator unit. After that, he made his report, and they went through the contents of the box while they waited for a reply.

Luckily, using the techpad Draknaroki dictionary, they were able to translate the label on a sealed container of feeding tubes right away. The baby was starting to show all the signs of being very hungry and about to be VERY upset over it. It took a little doing, and the fussy infant's lavender face was darkening to a bright purple as she scrunched it up and howled, but they were able to get a tube set up and ready to go. Both adults enjoyed the silence that ensued as Marie proceeded to feed her.

Colton stopped his work on the data device, and just sat there and watched his wife with the feeding baby in her arms. A soft smile grew in his eyes at the scene.

Just then, the indicator on the port the data device was plugged into beeped, and a translated recording began to play.

"*If you have find this talk, I dead. Care for small one I leave. My love/mate killed day past. Know not who. Fly over here. Beyond sight length. Take not small one to Draknaroke Prime. I give no name. Parents fail, small one be kill too. I place in . . . to save.*

Please love her, as do I."

Colton looked over at Marie. The tears flowing silently down her face reflected in his own eyes.

"Colt, they just gotta let us keep this little one!"

"I know, Babe, I know. I feel the same way. Just don't get you hopes up too much, okay?"

Marie wiped at her face and gave a sniff. "I'll try."

"You know I love you, right?" her husband asked.

Marie smiled and gave the waited for reply, "That's what keeps me goin'."

Just then, the translator unit indicated download complete and translated. Colton called in to report. The answer came back to bring the translator equipment, and ALL other finds back to the base ship.

Marie gave a weak smile, nodded and began gathering up all the baby paraphernalia and placed it back into the box. She was hampered somewhat by the small sleeping infant in her arms. Evidently, the baby had gotten her tummy full and was most content to take another nap. The young couple giggled their way through the clean-up with the help of the support techs. Since the techs were all Vlivlarian, their reaction to the infant was hard to gauge. This caused the young couple to be very quiet and slightly apprehensive as they all made their way back to the ship.

The Vlivlarian captain met them at the cargo hatch. Upon seeing the infant, he directed Marie to take her to the chief medical officer in sickbay immediately. He and the survey commander would take Colton to go over the translations of both the data unit and the larger data cache.

With a quick glance at her husband, Marie left to carry out her orders. The looks on both the captain and commander's faces did not give the young married couple much hope of being able to keep the baby, but it was so hard to read Vlivarian faces that they decided not to give up.

The Vlivarian doctor had slightly better parameters to go by than the Stafford's had on Draknaroki physiology, but the infant still came through with flying colors. Marie was pleased when the baby was returned to her care and took her back to their small quarters to await any final decisions there.

The survey commander listened to the data device recording before starting on the files from the control banks. She turned to Colton with what he took for a curious look.

"This infant you have found. Would you wish to take responsibility for its upbringing?"

Colton let out the breath he just realized he was holding. "Yes, Commander, we would very much appreciate that responsibility being given to us."

The commander gave the Vilvlarian equivalent of a smile and a brief nod. "You may go and so advise your life companion. We will notify you when we discover anything of interest from the files you have retrieved."

Colton barely remembered to give the correct answer and salute before hurrying back to their quarters to give Marie the good news.

Both Marie and the infant jumped when Colton burst into the room.

"Babe, we get to keep her!"

Marie's mouth dropped open in shock. "We do?" She snatched up the baby and rushed to give her husband a huge smile and kiss.

"You hear that, little bit? I get to be your mama after all!"

The baby answered their smiling faces with a serious look of her own.

"First order of business," Colton said as they all returned to their places on the bed. "What are we going to call her? 'Little bit' works in a pinch, but I doubt she will want to write that on her college applications. Do you know any good Draknaroki names?"

"We've been talking about that while we were waiting for you," Marie attempted to look as serious as the baby, but failed as the grin refused to leave her face. "I don't know any Draknaroki names, good or bad. I was thinking about making up one of our own. What do you think about Marlak'Muon? That is Draknaroki for 'small abandoned one'."

"I think it fits," Colton smiled down at the baby. "Well, Marlak'Muon, what do you think? Does that sound like a good name to you?"

Tears began running down Marie's cheeks and also filled Colton's eyes as the baby gave them her first tentative smile.

"I take that for a yes!" her new father laughed.

They spent the next two hours playing with and getting to know their new child. Marlak'Muon responded eagerly to the love they showed her, working her way even deeper into their hearts with every smile. Just then a bell tone sounded on the communications unit next to the bed. After a quick look at his wife, Colton reached over and punched the button.

"Data Retrieval/Technology Expert Colton Stafford and Linguistic/Cultural Specialist Marie Stafford please come to the main lounge immediately. Please bring the Draknaroki infant with you."

"Now what?" Marie asked as they got up and prepared to answer the summons.

"No idea," her husband answered with a thoughtful look. "Maybe they have gotten through the data files already. Let's go find out."

When they reached the lounge, they found that the entire survey crew had already assembled. The slight murmuring went silent as the Staffords took their seats, being the last to arrive. The Vlivlarian commander took her place beside the large techscreen at the head of the room.

"We have been able to retrieve the information held in the Draknaroki data cache, and have gone over all the preliminary data from all three scanning passes. I will now share the facts we know for certain at this time.

"The five structural remains that we discovered and were able to study were the control points for a base shield and cloaking system. This explains why we did not know of the outpost's existence until after it had been destroyed. It is also the reason that those five structures were not completely obliterated along with the rest of the base. Evidently, there was enough residual shield resonance to allow what little was left to remain."

She turned toward the young couple seated off to the right side of the room.

"Linguistic/Cultural Specialist Marie Stafford and Data Retrieval/Technology Expert Colton Stafford, will you please come to me."

With yet another set of questioning looks hastily thrown at each other, the couple complied.

The Vlivlarian commander reached for small Marlak'Muon, and held her for all the room to see, turning slowly so that each would have a full view of her tiny face before returning her to her new mother.

The commander placed her hand on the infant's curly head. "This is the ONLY survivor of the attack on the Draknaroki outpost. She was found in a small stasis unit beneath the central shield control building. Similar units were found under each of the outlying shield control buildings. Several had been occupied. All had been destroyed."

She stepped over and brought a data readout up on the main techscreen. "Here is a listing of what few Draknaroki remains we were able to find. They include male and female, young and old of each. Of all the remains we were able to catalog, we found only five percent were armored warriors with weapons. Ninety-five percent of all the remains discovered appear to be family units." She changed the readout display, and the new one slowly scrolled by, allowing all to read the findings as she resumed.

"These are the base records that Data Retrieval/Technology Expert Colton Stafford and Linguistic/Cultural Specialist Marie Stafford recovered from the main shield control building's data storage unit. They confirm all our preliminary findings concerning weapons emplacements or manufacturing facilities.

"There were none.

"This was indeed a research and development outpost. It was not, however, being used for weaponry of any kind. This was an agricultural and hydroponics research base.

"It appears Draknaroke Prime, along with several other planets in their system, is being threatened by extreme drought conditions. This base was being used to research ways to grow food to feed the Draknaroki people.

"The remains we have found were those of Draknaroki scientist and farmers, and their families."

A stunned silence met this revelation. The commander paused to give those assembled time to take it in before resuming.

"An agricultural research and development outpost was a 'threat' to the unknown forces who utterly and completely destroyed it."

Marie hugged Marlak'Muon up close to her chest as Colton wrapped his arms around both of them. Tears were streaming down not only their cheeks but also a large percentage of all those assembled.

The survey commander gave her audience a few moments to compose themselves. When she continued even her normally steady, cultured voice wavered. "We must now make all haste to return to the Space League of Worlds to reveal our findings to the ruling council. Any further study of this outpost must be accomplished at a later time.

"We must take steps to help the Draknaroki people, but our first step is clear. We MUST discover who the beings were who destroyed this outpost. After that, they MUST be stopped. No matter the cost."

As the strong arms holding her and the baby tightened ever so slightly, Marie looked up at Colton with a watery smile. She knew, even without him saying the words, that he felt exactly as she did. While finding the ones behind the destruction of the outpost might well be the first step the Space League needed to take, it was not theirs. Loving little Marlak'Muon was. They would protect and raise her, making sure that she knew as much about the Draknaroki people and their customs as possible. First and foremost though, Marlak'Muon, the small abandoned one, would always know that she was loved.

The Antiquarian

B. David Spicer

Fredrick Pierce's uncle Raymond passed away on the fifteenth day of March in the year 2108, but since Fred had never met the man and had only dimly been aware that he even had an uncle, he wasn't terribly upset. It would be more precise to say that Raymond had been his great-great uncle, and he was exactly one hundred and twenty years old when he died. By some quirk of fate he gave up the ghost on his 120th birthday.

So when Fred saw the message informing him of this sad event waiting in the message queue on his household system, he was mildly surprised, if not terribly upset. His uncle had, for some reason, made him executor of his will, a duty easily discharged since Raymond had left everything to his great-great nephew Fred. There was a smallish amount of money and some other personal items listed in the will.

Raymond had spent the last several decades of his life at the Regency Estates Retirement Community in Pittsburgh. Fred hadn't ever been to Pittsburgh, but he keyed in the contact information and was relieved to find that Raymond had dispossessed himself of most of his belongings in his final weeks. That meant that Fred wouldn't be responsible for paying for its disposal, and that was a relief.

"There is only one trunk of stuff left here, and it's been addressed to you Mr. Pierce," said the blue-haired nurse on the comlink.

"How much will it cost to ship? I mean, can't you have it recycled or something? You can keep the credits and everything." Fred just wanted to be done with this nonsense, his favorite net-show was coming on in moments, and his system had his music muted so low that he could barely hear it.

"The postage has been prepaid Mr. Pierce."

"Ok. Ship it or whatever. Thank you."

Fred severed the link and plunged into the vinylette comfort of his poly-foam filled couch. "Netlink active, channel 5078, sublink channels 2123, 4817, 1066 and 6982. Ambient music active, level two," he ordered the household system. Immediately the wall-screen snapped from standby mode to active mode, the large center portion displayed his favorite reality show, *Make It or Break It*, while four smaller screens displayed other programs. Music from the recent "Crunch" movement leapt in volume, and at last, in the midst of this glorious digital cacophony, Fredrick Pierce was able to relax.

He'd forgotten about Uncle Raymond's trunk until it arrived. Fred was in the kitchen selecting his dinner from the Auto Chef's menu when the household system announced the arrival of a package. He slapped the open door key and looked down at the dusty wooden box on the floor just outside his door. The delivery mech hadn't even waited for a confirmation and was already scuttling down the hall. "Hey! Thanks for bringing it inside! Idiotic buggy mechs!" Fred sighed as he bent over to pick up the box himself. It was heavy! "Let me guess, Uncle Raymond collected rocks!" He grumbled bitterly as he dragged the trunk through the door.

He got it far enough inside the room that the door stopped complaining and shut, then went to the kitchen to finish ordering his dinner before *Run For Your Life* came on. He loved that show! Since today was Tuesday, he had six sublink channels on in addition to *Run For Your Life*; most of them were digitally emulated sports events. Real people hadn't actually played sports in decades of course; they could hurt themselves after all, and with all the genetic enhancements available, it was too easy for humans to cheat. It would take someone as old as Uncle Raymond to remember when people would hit a ball with a bat and physically run the bases. Now-a-days the Central Net Sports System emulated all the old fashioned games using computer-generated players and randomized game conditions and events. Fred loved sports!

Uncle Raymond's trunk sat obtrusively on the floor of Fred's flat for days until he could stand it no more. It was a large wooden box painted flat black, though it was so dusty that it seemed more gray than black. Its brass hinges and lock were black with tarnish and accumulated filth. If someone had wanted to place an object that would completely clash with the tidy, clean digital decor of Fred's apartment, the trunk would have been what they would have chosen. Cursing, he dragged the trunk into the living room and sat in his posh vinylette couch. He keyed in the security code that the retirement center had provided him with into the antique analog lock and opened the lid. Immediately a strange, musty odor assaulted his nostrils and he nearly gagged.

"Airflow, maximum!" he called out, and the household system obligingly pumped out the offending air. He peered into the box, still pinching his nose. Uncle Raymond had sent his nephew a trunk full of books. Fred squinted at some of the titles: *Arabian Nights*, *Walden*, and *The Count of Monte Cristo*. Each leather-bound volume looked downright ancient. Fred had rarely seen books before, though you could still find them sometimes on auction sites, or even in antique malls, but he'd never seen a leather-bound book, indeed he'd never seen real leather. The books were stacked four high, so there must have been fifty books in the trunk.

Fred gingerly lifted one out of the trunk and turned it over in his hands. The cover was a rich brown and had a grainy, not unpleasant texture. The thought that he was holding the skin of a dead animal in his hands made Fred's stomach churn acidly, but he couldn't deny his interest. He carefully opened the cover; the paper of each page was a rich cream color. The text was static, printed in old-fashioned hardcopy. He read the words out loud, "It was the best of times, it was the worst of times."

Time slipped away as Fred read. The net-shows careened across his wall-screen, his "Crunch" music favorites droned on, track after track after track, and still he read. The words on the page did not blink, or scroll, or dance around demanding his attention. They stood motionless but still told a story. And what a story it was! It was set centuries before, during a period of history that he vaguely recalled spending a day studying once when he a child. His tutor mech might have mentioned it during the chapter on Europe. If Europe was important enough to rate an entire chapter in his tutor's static memory, then certainly something as seemingly important as the French Revolution must have been mentioned, right? Fred wasn't sure, but the story captivated him. When he at last closed the book, he looked up and saw the time.

"What?" He stared at the chronometer and gasped. "I missed all my net-shows, all of them!" That hadn't ever happened before, not once since he was a child. Fred stood there, staring blankly at the chronometer and he remembered the story the book told him. He recalled how alive the characters had seemed, he recalled seeing the story play out on the wall-screen of his mind, and he was suddenly glad he'd missed *Make It Or Break It* and his virtual sports league would inevitably play another game tomorrow. With a smile on his face, Fredrick Pierce went to bed

* * * *

The auto-chef gurgled his coffee into a mug and spat out nutritionally balanced bacon and egg analogues onto his plate. Fred checked his message queue while he ate, but an incoming comlink popped open on his screen. Gary Burns, who lived several floors above, smiled from the wall-screen.

"What did you think of the game, huh? Chicago's going to the Series for sure, right?"

Fred munched his bacon analogue. "I didn't watch it, sorry."

"You didn't even sublink it? Man oh man, what could be more important than the game? Were you watching the mech races or something?"

"No, I, ah, was reading," said Fred.

Gary looked confused. "Reading what? Not that new show with the puzzles and the android chick?"

Fred rolled his eyes. "No, Gary, I was reading a book!"

"A book? You mean on that new interactive channel?"

"I mean a book, hardcopy, you know paper pages, no power supply, no scrolling text, no explosions."

Gary looked more confused. "Why?"

"It was something new to do, okay?"

Gary's eyes bulged as he said, "But you are gonna watch the game tonight, right? I mean it's Chicago and Cincinnati! Cincinnati!"

Fred had to smile. Despite his endless ability to multitask, Gary was truly a creature with a one-track mind. "I don't know, Gary. To be honest I might read another book tonight."

Gary looked stricken. "And miss another game? Look, couldn't you just sublink it while your book thingy is on the main link? It's Cincinnati!"

Fred sighed. "I'll think about it all right?"

Gary broke into a wide grin. "You'll watch it—nobody misses two games! I'll talk to you later, okay?" Gary severed the link before Fred could reply.

Fred finished his breakfast and went into the living room. The musty smell was back, and he found that it was much less unpleasant today. He sat on the couch and looked into the trunk. The richly appointed tomes were still there. He reached out his hand and selected one at random. He would have to go to work tomorrow, but he had today all to himself. He flipped through the book wondering if the awe he experienced last night was a fluke, or would this book carry him away as well? He read aloud the first sentence of the second book he had ever in his life read, "Dorothy lived in the midst of the great Kansas prairies, with Uncle Henry, who was a farmer, and Aunt Em, who was the farmer's wife."

* * * *

Workdays were always miserable. Usually Fred was grateful when his workweek ended, but even though today was only the beginning of the week, he whistled while he walked down the hall and smiled as he coded invoices and manipulated data. Today his body was at work, but his mind was in Oz. It had surprised him to realize that he knew the story that the book kept between its pages. It had been made into net-shows a time or two, but the images that the stationary words on the crinkly pages evoked were infinitely more detailed and sublime than any pixilated panorama churned out by the net-studios. Even a day after reading the story, he could still see it playing out in his mind, and it made him smile.

Gary Burns was also at work today, and he showed up at Fred's desk right on schedule, looming as it were, like an evil Kalidah on the road of yellow brick.

"Well, it's a sure bet now, right?"

"Hmmm?" Fred tapped his keyboard and stared at the holo-display, not particularly interested in talking to Gary at the moment.

"The Cubs in the series—you think it's a sure bet now, right? I mean that line drive that Swithin cracked in the third! Wow!"

"Gary, you do realize that there is no Swithin, right? Swithin is just a computer generated fantasy that a computer in Chicago uses to play against a computer in Cincinnati. Tell me you know that those aren't real people?"

Gary looked hurt. "What's wrong with you today? Are they working you too hard or what?"

"No, it's just that I don't care if Chicago goes to the Series anymore. I haven't watched a game in days. In *days*, Gary." Fred continued working, but Gary didn't take the hint.

"Not even on sublink?"

"Nope, not even on sublink."

"I don't get it, you used to always watch Chicago play. You got a new team or something?"

"Not at all, I just don't watch baseball anymore. As a matter of fact, I haven't watched vids or net-shows all week, well since Friday, anyway."

Gary squinted at Fred suspiciously. "You got a neural link, didn't you? Man, how did you afford one of those? My wife would kill me, just kill me!" Gary craned his head behind Fred's own, looking for the neural port on the back of his skull. "They say the games you can play through one of those is just amazing! They pump the vid-stream right into the brain!"

Fred sighed deeply. "Gary, I did *not* get a neural-link." He tried to rub the imminent headache out of his forehead. "I was reading, if you must know!"

"Again? I thought you did that already. Why did you have to do it again?"

"I read a different book, numbskull." Fred scowled at Gary before returning to his data manipulation.

"Where did you even get hardcopy books anyway? I've never even seen one." Gary scratched his head while his unibrow furrowed.

"My uncle left me some. He died last week."

"Well, sorry about your uncle and all, but that's no excuse for beating me up is it?"

"Gary, I'm not beating you up okay? I just haven't been watching sports, and I don't feel like talking about baseball. You understand, right?" Fred said it slowly, as if he were speaking to a child.

"Sure, Fred, whatever you say. Oh, Maddie is having some of her friends over tomorrow for dinner because she bought a new recipe upgrade for the auto-chef and she wants to try it out. She said I could have a guest too. Wanna come?" Gary looked eager, like a child on Christmas morning, expectant and hopeful, and suddenly Fred felt very sorry for him.

"All right, what time?"

You'd have thought he'd just been made Emperor of the cosmos the way Gary's face lit up.

"Seven thirty, hey I'll see you then!" He loped away with his waggling hand in the air.

"That man needs to see the Wizard worse than the Scarecrow ever did." Fred chuckled and whistled another lively tune.

Later that night Fred selected another book and settled in on his couch to read it. His workday had been long and tedious, and reading would be his reward. As he opened the cover and admired the drawing of a man with the odd name of Sherlock Holmes, he was suddenly annoyed by the noises the vidlinks were making. "Vid-link volume, minimum level. Sever all sublinks, ambient music, minimum level." The sounds receded but never completely abated. "Vidlink off." He tried out the words but he'd never used that command before.

"Unable to comply. Restate command." The household system almost sounded annoyed.

"Ambient music mute, vidlink mute."

"Unable to comply. Restate command."

"Just turn the entire net-feed off!"

"Unable to comply. Restate command."

"Open 'Help Center' link." Fred paced across the room in frustration.

A Help Center attendant called out in a cheery, artificial voice. "Hello, thank you for using Help Center. How may I assist you?"

"My vidlink won't power off. I need to know the quit command."

"Please clarify query. Define 'off.'"

Fred sighed in exasperation. "I want to terminate the feed from the vidlink and the music-link as well, how do I do that?"

"If you are relocating to a new domicile, the Entertainment Consortium will automatically transfer your entertainment preferences to your new location upon your registration with the Central Computer. You do not need to do anything. Thank you for using Help Center. Have a nice day."

"That's not what I asked!" Fred clenched his fists and made a face.

He looked at the wall-screen as if for the first time. It took up the entire surface of one wall of his flat. The opposite side of that wall faced into his bedroom, where another wall-screen stretched from floor to ceiling. He'd lived in this flat for seven years and couldn't remember a time when there wasn't at least one active vidlink. Even when he slept it droned on, quieter but still present. He'd read a word in one of the books that he'd had to look up: silence. He'd never heard the sound of silence, and now he definitely wanted to.

He knelt down and opened the little maintenance hatch at the bottom of the wall-screen. It was generally only used by maintenance mechs during hardware upgrades. Fred poked around in there for a few minutes until he found what he thought was the feed cable from the power trunk. Using a knife from the kitchen he slowly began to saw the cable. The plastic knife blade wasn't meant for this kind of work, so it was slow going. When the blade was halfway through the cable, a warning message began to blare from the wall-screen, "Your entertainment system is experiencing a hardware malfunction. Please be patient as a repair mech will arrive shortly." The knife finally cut through the cable and the wall-screen died.

He sat up and listened. For a moment he couldn't hear anything, except for a vague ringing in his ears. Was this silence? Not exactly. He could hear the sound of his neighbor's wall-screens seeping through the walls, and the techno-thump of dance music wafting down from the ceiling. Even with this noise pollution it was still eerily quiet by comparison. It was an unusual experience but the change was indeed welcome.

Then the household system announced that a repair mech sat waiting in the hall. Exasperated, Fred stood up and threw the dull knife into the kitchen, where the automaid dashed from its socket to retrieve it. "Deny entry." He'd never denied a repair mech entry before.

"Mech repair schedule requested." The household system brought up a scheduling menu on the little screen by the door.

"Deny request." The mech must have left then because the household system held its peace. Fred picked up his book and reclined on his couch. Dr. Watson had just arrived at the Baskerville estate when the doorbell chimed. "Who is it?"

"It's Wilkins, the building superintendent."

Sighing, Fred went to the door and slapped the open key. Mr. Wilkins was a middle-aged man with a completely shaved head and the unsettling stare of cybernetic eyes. "What can I do for you Mr. Wilkins?" Fred tried to smile, but he thought he knew why Wilkins was here.

"Well, sir, the building's maintenance system reported a wall-screen failure in your flat, and dispatched a repair mech to fix it. The mech returned and reported that it was unable to gain entry. I thought maybe it might be glitching or something, but the diagnostic I ran came back clean. So I thought I'd come up and see if there was a problem with your household system that I couldn't see from the maintenance network."

"There is no problem Mr. Wilkins, I severed the power to the wall-screen."

Wilkins looked bewildered. "You severed the power?"

"Yes."

"On purpose?"

"Yes!" Fred felt his temper growing short.

"Why would you want to do that?" Wilkins' electronic eyes clicked as he narrowed his vision to study Fred's face.

"I tried to turn it off, but the system didn't recognize the commands, so I severed the power. End of story."

"Right. Well, when would it be convenient for the repair mech to come reattach the power? If we do it now we can have the wall-screen back online before *Political Arena* comes on." He tilted his head and tried to see into the flat.

"Mr. Wilkins, I don't think I'll want the wall-screen repaired anytime soon, so your repair-mech minions can safely stay in their recharge sockets. Thank you very much for stopping by." Fred tossed Wilkins a jaunty salute as slapped the strike plate to close the door.

"Mr. Pierce, wait a moment." He wedged his foot in the door. "I feel I must warn you that I have received several complaints from your neighbors in the last few hours."

It was Fred's turn to look confused. "Complaints? About what?"

"Well, sir, the quiet."

"The quiet?"

"Yes, the sounds from your wall-screen and other audio systems all went dead when you severed the power. The quiet has been polluting your neighbors' flats. Every one of them has had to adjust their own audio systems to compensate. It has caused them serious inconvenience."

Fred's jaw hung open and he said nothing for several seconds. "That is ridiculous! They'll just have to get used to it."

Wilkins might have looked uncomfortable then, but his metallic eyes made it hard to tell. "Sir, if I can't get you to allow a repair mech to reconnect your wall-screen, I fear that I won't have a choice but to notify the authorities."

"Notify them of what? That I want some quiet? What crime have I committed?" Fred shouted at Wilkins, as if volume could break through ignorance.

"I'm not a police officer sir, but I believe you have seriously disturbed the peace on this floor. Mr. Kennedy, as you might recall, was fined for disturbing the peace last year."

Lucas Kennedy was an old man who had lost all of his body below the ribcage in the war. His cybernetics were antiquated and even more obviously mechanical than Wilkins' eyes. His lower body was a rough approximation of human form so he simply decided that with nothing to be modest about, he didn't need to wear trousers anymore. He was eventually arrested and fined, and made to see that he had to wear trousers, because that is simply what one did. Fred seethed in fury that Wilkins would even compare the current situation with Kennedy's pants.

"Look here, Wilkins, I wanted some quiet, and now I have it. I'm going back inside my flat to read a book. You keep your mechs out, or else I'll be the one calling the authorities. Silence isn't a crime, harassment is. Is that clear?"

Wilkins' eyes clicked and whirled in their sockets, without another word, he turned and left.

Fred sat down heavily on his couch. His mood was sour and he found it difficult to read. He stared at the blank surface of his wall-screen, which seemed to stare at him. Fred closed his eyes and listened carefully. He could still hear the sounds of his neighbors' wall-screens. The sounds were louder than before, but compared to the usual sonic onslaught, it was unsettlingly still. Which is what he had wanted all along. Fred opened his book and read.

* * * *

Hundreds of people bustled around the galleria this morning, each intent on purchasing some new bauble that they saw on the vids last night or had the need for some item subtly implanted in their brain by their wall-screen while they slept. Fred however, was looking for something different.

It had occurred to him that his selection of books was finite and at the rate he was reading them he'd run out of unread books in a few weeks. So he'd come to this twenty-story temple of conspicuous consumerism in the hopes of finding some. Most of the stores in the mall peddled the usual mix of goods, clothing, jewelry, high tech gizmos and toys, but there were a handful of odd-ball antique shops, nano-fiber tattoo parlors, and meat-shops where you could get "replacement hearts while you wait!"

The first antique store he tried had many interesting things like prewar hologram projectors whose images looked quaintly old-fashioned, and even computers so ancient that they still had processors gauged in petabytes. No books to be found though. The second shop had a data chip with a "virtual bookshelf" on it that turned out to be a selection of old net-shows from two decades ago. Strangely the shop also had a pair of L-shaped plastic sculptures shaped like eagles called ‘bookends’. Fred had to ask what they were for, but the clerk, a nubile young woman who had obviously already started the inevitable genetic body-upgrade, had no clue. He bought them anyway.

At the third shop he tried, Fred hit the jackpot. He found a large rack of shelves in the back of the store that held hundreds of books. They were definitely books, but they were somewhat different that Uncle Raymond’s books. The former were large hardback, leather-bound books with creamy white pages, the latter were smaller with softly flexible covers that had illustrations on them. The overall quality was lower, and they seemed to have been made at a time subsequent to Raymond’s collection of books. But they were still books, and Fred wanted them. The prices were much less than he expected, so he eagerly began selecting what he hoped were the best of the bunch.

At the checkout counter Fred described his uncle’s books to the old man who was working it. The clerk’s eyes lit up. “The books you’re describing are probably a century and a half old or more. I myself have a modest collection of books from that era.”

“How many do you have?”

“Nearly ten.” The old man puffed up proudly. “You?”

“I have fifty-three.”

The clerk’s jaw dropped open. “That must have cost you a fortune. Why do you need these paperbacks when you have so many hardbacks?”

“I’m afraid that I’ll read all of my, what did you call them? Hardbacks? I want to have more books to read when I’m done with my hardbacks, and these paperbacks are all that I’ve been able to find.”

"I've never read any of mine. I just like having them around."

Fred stared at the old man. "You should try it. You might be surprised by how much you like it."

"Well, I do sublink the 'Literature Channel.'"

"Ah well, good for you." Fred scooped up his new books and left the store. The clerk called after him "Come back when you want to sell those hardbacks!"

"Count on it." Fred didn't even look back.

* * * *

The moment Fred rushed through the door of his flat and dropped his burden of books onto the table, the household network began spouting off a list of messages, all from Gary reminding him of the dinner party that Maddie was hosting this evening. Fred had almost completely forgotten about the party, and glancing at the chronometer he saw that it was nearly seven o'clock now. He groaned loudly. He wouldn't have time to read until after dinner. He dashed into the shower and afterwards haphazardly threw on the first suit of clothes he found.

Gary and Maddie lived in the same building as Fred, just eleven floors up. Their flat was considerably larger than his own and furnished with much more extravagance. Their wall-screen, one of the new high-resolution models with holographic image projectors for deep immersion entertainment, yammered away across the room. It covered the entirety of three walls in the living room, and the smaller screens in the other rooms were nearly as large as Fred's own disabled main wall-screen. The scent of ozone hung ever-present in their flat, and Fred could smell it now as Gary greeted him at the door.

"Fred! Glad you could make it, come on in." Gary pumped Fred's hand and grinned like a loon. Fred stepped through the door and saw the electronic bacchanalia of lit up gizmos and the fullest expression of technological excess that he'd ever witnessed. Maddie wasn't interested in "keeping up with the Jones's," as the old saying went; she was intent on showing them up. Fred knew that Gary worked extra shifts several days a week, and that Maddie herself worked a few days every week just to pay for their lifestyle, though Maddie would sooner die than admit it. She liked to claim that she was the scion of an old-money family from "back east." Between them they earned more money than Fred did by several orders of magnitude, but they also worked well beyond what modern society found acceptable, so they were forced to keep their supplemental incomes a secret and live lies every bit as extravagant as their furniture. Looking around the flat, Fred made note of all the changes since his last visit, new couch-massage, new nanoprint wallpaper on the one wall not covered by the wall-screens, new ultra-plush carpeting, crystal polymer chandelier.

"The other guests are already here," Gary said as he led Fred into the dining room. To hear Maddie tell it, the people milling about the table should be called "Titans of Industry," but Fred thought that none of these people qualified as Titans of anything. He recognized Reginald Towley from past dinner parties. He liked to say he was CEO of a software firm that made third-party upgrades to auto-maid mechs. He neglected to mention that he was also the only employee of his business and that every major auto-maid manufacturer recommended that their clients not use his upgrades. He stood by the window dressed in a silver pinstriped suit that cinched a bit too tightly around the middle and had a walrus-like mustache that fluttered like a flag whenever he spoke. He tittered away to a woman wrapped in a blue gown of some vaguely metallic weave who had her hair up in a complicated sculpture of bows and tassels. This woman was Eugenia Kane, granddaughter of Dr. Franklin Kane who had found the cure for cancer, and the ex-wife of Reyes Mariposa, the B-list actor. Today, she pretended to be an important socialite who always got invited to all the best parties. In Fred's opinion, the woman hadn't done a single thing of consequence in her own right during her life. She clung to the memory of her grandfather and ex-husband's dubious fame, and to hear her tell it, their accomplishments couldn't have happened without her assistance. Fred thought she should have kept her ex-husband's last name.

At the far side of the room was a woman with all of the physical beauty that money could buy. A vivid vision of perfection wrapped in a form fitting red dress, her name was Madeline Dumont, a model who had been posing for pictures for over thirty years, but because of her never-ending gene modification (colloquially known as meat-modding) she looked barely eighteen. Her flawless doe eyes quickened the pulse of too many men to mention, but looking at her now, when no cameras were present, her gaze was so emptily vapid that she looked like a child's plastic doll. Her handlers had managed to build a cosmetic empire for themselves based on her engineered good looks and had become billionaires several times over. Unfortunately Madeline had signed her modeling contract when she really was as young as she now looked and got paid barely enough to buy the cosmetics and modding that her pictures sold. Gary's wife Maddie thought it quite cute that she shared a name with such a renowned model.

The only person Fred didn't recognize was an older man who dressed simply but elegantly in a dark suit and was nearly bald. Baldness wasn't common anymore—any discount meat-shop could cure baldness—and so it surprised Fred when he saw the man. He stood alone, looking out of a window with an empty martini glass in his hand.

Maddie came gliding into the room dressed in a shockingly blue gown, obviously expensive and meant to look it. She greeted each guest politely and chatted them up saying, "Oh, how lovely you look" and "Madeline, my dear, you are a vision."

To Fred she simply grunted, "Hello Fred," which summed up what she'd likely say to him during the whole evening. Maddie didn't like one inch of Fred, and he felt the same way about her. She only tolerated his presence because he was her husband's only friend. Gary looked exquisitely uncomfortable and spoke only to Fred. Maddie had probably told him to keep quiet. The guests had little holographic placards on the table indicating their seats. Gary and Fred were placed as far away from Maddie as possible.

The auto-maid units began bringing steaming dishes of food to the table and Maddie motioned everyone to sit. Fred looked at his plate; it contained some sort of sauce-covered dish—he couldn't tell if it was chicken or fish—and a little mound of seasoned rice. It smelled strongly of curry and pepper. Fred carved off a bit and stuck it into his mouth. It tasted, as he suspected, very spicy and more than a little hot. He forced himself to chew and swallow, his eyes watering and his sinuses opening up.

He looked around the table and he saw the same reaction on all the guests' faces. The flavor surprised them all, as the spicy heat of the sauce scorched their palates. But then Fred witnessed something truly amazing. They guests all began to congratulate Maddie on her culinary skills.

"Maddie, this meal is simply divine! I wish I had your skill in the kitchen!" Eugenia Kane indicated her meal with a wave of her wine glass.

Madeline Dumont bobbled her head up and down. "I'll have to get this recipe; it really is just too delectable."

Reginald Towley made a show of gobbling up his chicken (or fish). "If my fourth wife could cook like that, I'd have stayed married to her!" He roared with laughter, obviously a fan of his own humor.

Fred noticed that the bald man hadn't taken more than one bite, and he had a mild look of disgust on his face. Gary leaned to Fred whispered loud enough that Maddie could hear him. "Good, isn't it Fred?"

Before Fred could answer, Maddie called out to the bald man, "Don't you like it, Uncle Devon?"

The bald man looked at Maddie with a downturned mouth. "It is quite spicy."

"Yes, it is. Exquisitely so." Maddie smiled as if Uncle Devon had just offered a compliment. "It is quite difficult to get just right, but I seem to have managed." The gaggle of guests nodded their assent, all except Devon who continued to scowl at his plate and Fred who felt suddenly that he was at a tea party in Wonderland.

Gary chomped loudly and swallowed noisily. Fred whispered to Gary, "She didn't cook this crap did she? She used the auto-chef right?" Gary had a mouth full of food but nodded his head.

"You have an opinion, Mr. Pierce?" Maddie called from the head of the table, looking less than pleased.

"Well, yes, I suppose I do. You didn't cook this food. The auto-chef cooked it, the auto-maids served it, and they will clean up afterward."

Every eye pinned him to his seat, and from the corner of his eye, Fred could see Gary crumble next to him.

"I don't understand, Mr. Pierce." Maddie spoke in a tone that stated unequivocally she definitely did understand. "What do you mean?"

"Well, it seems to me that we should all be complimenting the auto-chef on a job well done, and perhaps thanking the auto-maids for keeping our wine glasses full so we can put out the inferno that your dinner ignited in our mouths. I mean, it's a little silly for us to be complimenting you for cooking a meal that you didn't cook."

Her face collapsed into a scowl. "I secured the auto-chef upgrade, I selected the menu, I ordered the raw materials. What more is there to do?" Maddie's voice dripped condescension with every syllable.

By this time, Fred was getting annoyed. "Yes, Maddie, I don't doubt that you did all of those things, but you didn't cut up the fish—"

"Chicken!"

"All right, chicken then. You didn't add the spices; you didn't even boil the rice. How then can you say that you cooked the meal?"

Maddie had turned a harsh shade of red, darkening rapidly to purple. Most of the rest of the guests looked confused, but Devon had a small smirk on his face as he watched Fred. Madeline Dumont spoke up to defend Maddie, "Sir, who has time for all of that nonsense? Only a beast would expect a lady to go through all of that! Nobody would want poor little Maddie to do any such sort of thing."

She smiled at Maddie and nodded as if the conversation were over.

Reginald Towley's head was bobbing as Madeline spoke, his whiskers snapping back and forth. "In today's world, who wants to waste their time slaving away in the kitchen? My company is on the cutting edge of auto-chef upgrades, and even though this particular upgrade came from Cuisine King, a third-rate hack in my opinion, there is still no cause to ask anyone to do it the old fashioned way."

Maddie's fierce gaze had left Fred to glare at Towley for a moment, the "third-rate hack" comment having redirected her ire.

"There is something to be said for the old-fashioned way of doing things." Fred poked at his rice with his fork.

"Like what?"

"Like turning off the net-shows, like cooking your own food by hand, like reading a book."

"Not that again!" Gary threw up his hands and shook his head.

Maddie heard the anguish in her husband's words and latched onto what he had to say as ammunition. "Excuse me, what did you say darling?"

"Um, well dear, Fred, that is Mr. Pierce, has been reading."

"Reading what, darling?"

"Books. Hardcopy books." Fred said it before Gary could answer. "Real old-fashioned books."

Maddie looked delighted, the rest of the guests looked confused. Devon grinned a little grin.

Gary didn't hesitate to throw Fred to the wolves. "He even, uh, turned off his wall-screen."

There was a collective gasp. "Why would you do that? Won't you miss the net-shows?" Eugenia Kane clutched at her chest, as if fearing for her heartbeat.

"He must mean that he watches the 'Literature Channel' but sublinks everything else." Madeline Dumont said it with a condescending smile.

"No, I really turned the whole feed off, no net-shows, no music feed, no vidlinks, no sublinks. Nothing at all," said Fred with a smile.

Maddie had a wicked grin on her face. "I think Mr. Pierce, that you have an interesting hobby, but one that could get you labeled a Luddite."

Fred shrugged. "If the shoe fits, I'll wear it. I have nothing to be ashamed of."

Devon turned to him. "How did you turn off the net-feed?"

"I physically severed the link."

"Indeed?" Devon looked pensive.

"I must admit, Mr. Pierce, that your outlook on the world is bad for business. Very bad indeed!" Mr. Towley huffed through his whiskers.

"How so?"

"Well, sir, I spend good money on advertising, good hard-earned money. It is your *duty* to see to it that my money isn't wasted."

"Excuse me? How is it that I have a duty to watch your commercials?"

"How can I stay in business if people won't watch net-shows? I need to get my product out there so people can see what I have to offer. If they are fool enough to sever their link and read books all day, they won't ever see my commercials! I spend a fortune on flashy commercials."

"Perhaps you should spend more money on building a quality product instead. That way when I buy one of your upgrades I'll tell all my friends about how great it is so they can buy it too."

Reginald Towley laughed loudly, pounding his meaty fist on the table. "The man is insane."

"What? Is it insane to expect a quality product from a manufacturer? Or is it insane to want something better for myself than sitting around all day eyes glued to a wall-screen watching *Political Arena* or simulated baseball?"

"Yes, those things are insane. And so are you, Mr. Pierce." Maddie said it in a tone that concluded the conversation. The auto-maids served dessert, a chocolate mousse, and conversation drifted away to more Maddie-centric topics. Fred noticed that Maddie carefully avoided his eye and he suspected that Gary would be punished later for inviting him. The moment the party moved into the living room, Fred excused himself. At the door Devon stopped him and shook his hand.

"It was a pleasure meeting you, Mr. Pierce. I suspect we'll see each other soon." Over Devon's shoulder he caught the icy glare of Maddie's disdain. Fred smiled.

His smile stayed on his face as he walked to the lift, and he whistled as he approached his flat. Then he noticed the police officers.

"Mr. Pierce? I'm officer Danner and this is officer Quan. We'd like to speak to you regarding your net-feed." Officer Danner possessed an Olympian physique, likely the result of copious genetic mods. The Asian woman next to him stood tall and lean, with the body language of a trained fighter. Fred just sighed.

"I confess, I severed the feed. I don't want it anymore."

Officer Danner looked confused. "Am I to understand that you are admitting your crime?"

"I admit to severing the net-feed. I didn't know that that was a crime. I don't see how it can be a crime."

"It's vandalism at best, but I think a case could be made for felonious tampering with a public utility. I think you'd better come with us."

"This is insanity! All I wanted was some quiet so I could read!" Fred hissed in exasperation as they placed handcuffs on his wrists and led him to the lift.

The officers led him out of the lift and down the concrete steps in front of the building. Mr. Wilkins, the building superintendent, stood outside the door watching Fred being led away like a criminal toward the waiting police cruiser. His metallic eyes whirred and clicked and his lips twisted into a self-satisfied smile.

The trip to the police station wasn't long. Neither officer said a word to Fred, and he himself remained silent.

He kept running the last few days through his mind. Had he committed a crime? Was it really a crime to want to turn off the wall-screen? Maybe so, that would explain why there wasn't an "off" command or a power switch. Fred lowered his head into his cuffed hands and resigned himself to despair.

The local police station, a windowless concrete cube, squatted gracelessly across three city-blocks. Fred saw a jungle of antennas and dishes sprouting from the roof, but he lost sight of them as the cruiser turned into the mouth of the tunnel that led to the station's underground parking facility. They led Fred through a glass doorway and into the station. Under the harsh glare of fluorescent light, officers keyed in data or escorted their prisoners to holding cells. Officers Danner and Quan led him through a labyrinth of desks to a corner where Officer Danner seated him across the desk from a cluttered computer terminal.

"Well now, Mr. Pierce, you have already admitted that you intentionally severed your net-feed, correct?" Danner glared at him, but Fred only nodded. "You also refused to allow said net-feed to be repaired by the building's repair mech, correct?" Fred nodded again.

"You do realize what penalty a felony charge carries, right?" asked Officer Quan.

"No, I don't. I still don't even see what crime I have committed. I just got sick of all the noise. I ordered the household system to turn it off, but it couldn't. What was I supposed to do?"

"That's a great question, what were you going to do with no net-feed? You couldn't watch any net-shows or play any video games. What were you going to do?" Officer Danner's tone seemed to imply that he thought Fred might be up to something nefarious.

"I already told you, I wanted to read."

Officer Danner's face split into with a triumphant grin. "Ha! Gotcha! How could you even receive a book without a net-feed?"

"I don't need to download anything to read. I have several books of my own. My uncle died and I inherited his books, and I've found a few at antique stores."

"You mean hard-copy books? Made out of paper?" Officer Quan sounded incredulous.

"Yes."

"And reading these books led you to committing the crime?" Officer Danner pecked at the keyboard, entering the facts of Fred's transgression.

"If you mean did I sever the net-feed to facilitate my reading, then yes. Though I still don't think I've committed any crime."

"You know that your neighbors filed complaints with your building superintendent, right?"

"Wilkins mentioned something about that. That without my wall-screen's sound system blasting through the walls it was too quiet. I didn't realize that it was my responsibility to create noise just to keep my neighbors happy!" Fred's annoyance crept into his raised voice.

"All right, calm down, Mr. Pierce. This attitude isn't helping your case any. We all have a responsibility to society, but you don't seem to take yours seriously." Officer Danner gave him a frown.

"Officer Danner, let me see if I understand you correctly. Are you telling me that I have a social obligation to sit in my living room and watch the wall-screen every waking minute of every day, with the volume at such a level that it bleeds through the walls into the surrounding flats? Is that what you mean to say? What if I don't want to watch the wall-screen all the time? Don't I have the right to turn it off when I want to? If not, who took that right away from me?"

The officers looked amused. "There are over fifty-thousand channels available in the basic net package, with all those options you couldn't find anything you liked to watch? So you had to read?" Officer Quan chuckled, obviously amused.

Fred sighed in exasperation. "Look, I didn't *have* to read, I *wanted* to read. And to answer your question, yes there were shows I liked, but I just don't want to watch them any more."

"Why not?"

"I like reading better."

Both officers looked at Fred as if he had lobsters falling out of his nose. "You like reading better than watching net-shows?"

"Yes."

"Well, I think I've heard enough. These books of yours led you to commit a crime. I think we should probably confiscate them before they cause you to commit another one." Officer Danner summoned a holo-cam to take a mugshot of Fred. "Should we petition to have books placed on the contraband items list, Quan?"

"Probably should. They drove this guy insane."

Officer Danner nodded and began keying in the contraband request. "It never ceases to amaze me how messed up some people are. Booze. Drugs. Illegal meat-upgrades. Books. It's just disgusting."

Fred stared off into space, but became aware of a figure approaching from across the sea of desks. It was a bald man dressed in a dark suit, and he looked familiar. Eventually he realized the man was Maddie's Uncle Devon.

"Good evening gentlemen." Devon gave a curt nod to Officers Danner and Quan.

Officer Danner stood as Devon approached. "Inspector Regents, how can we help you?" Fred's eyes widened as he looked at Devon.

"Well, boys, a delivery truck just collided with a construction mech about three blocks away. I need you to go help reroute traffic and handle crowd control."

"Well sir, we were just booking this man here . . ." Quan's voice trailed off.

"Oh, I'll take care of that. Crowd control must be your priority right now." Devon shooed the two officers out the door. He sat down in the chair across from Fred and smiled.

"I told you that we'd see each other soon."

"Inspector?" asked Fred.

"Yes, I guess I am, but to Maddie I'm 'Uncle Devon.'" He scanned the computer screen in front of him. "So, let's see, what are you being charged with, vandalism, and oh my, tampering with a public utility. Danner has also recommended that you be referred to the psychiatric ward for a full evaluation. Tsk, tsk, tsk." Devon shook his head sadly.

Fred sat up strait in his chair. "He thinks I'm insane?"

"I'm afraid so. Are you?"

Fred hung his head. "I don't know anymore. Maybe I am."

"I don't think you are, Fred." Devon leaned across the desk towards him. "I'll tell you a secret—I like to read books too."

Fred's eyes widened and his jaw hung open.

"It's true." Devon chuckled. "There are a few of us around."

Fred closed his eyes and took a deep breath. "Thank you. I thought I was all alone."

"Oh you're certainly not alone, Fred, but people like us, we are in the minority these days. Most people in our society have become mindless slaves to their wall-screens. They watch their favorite shows, sometimes a dozen or more sublinked at a time, record them, and discuss them with their friends, neighbors and coworkers. They are so trapped in the cycle of programming that they have forgotten that there is another way of living. So when people like you or I come along, well, they just don't understand us at all."

Fred listened carefully and nodded his head in agreement.

"Reading isn't extinct, but it is on the Endangered Species List. There are still people who read, but we represent a smaller proportion of the population every year. They haven't banned books because they don't need to. The percentage of people who read books is now so small that banning books would only increase interest in them, hence it would be counterproductive." Devon sighed. "Though I see Danner has requested that books be declared contraband."

"Who would want them banned anyway? I mean besides Officer Danner. And why?"

"The people in charge are afraid of people who think. The government worries about people who think too much, advertisers don't want us to think about their products, just to buy them. Positions of power are dependent on the sanction of the less powerful; otherwise you have revolution and war. So the government and their media cronies mollify the masses with endless hours of net-shows that entertain without forcing anybody to think. The result is that the population is so distracted by entertainment programming that they fail to see how corrupt the system has become, and the bureaucrats get to stay in power."

Devon looked at Fred and smiled. "Then people like you come along, reading books, severing net-feeds and ruining dinner parties! Maddie will never forgive you. You'll probably never be invited to one of her parties again. For shame!"

"Oh no!" Fred grinned.

"There isn't much I can do about that." Devon's demeanor became serious. "I can, however, drop these ridiculous charges Danner has levied against you." He manipulated the data on the holo-display. "Vandalism? I think not." A large section of text disappeared from the display. "Disturbing the peace? Begone!" The entire entry for Frederick Pierce vanished from the display.

"I don't know how to thank you, Inspector."

"Your freedom comes with a price, I'm afraid."

Fred's brow furrowed. "A price? What kind of price?"

"Nothing difficult, but these terms are not negotiable. I'm insisting on them because I want to keep you out of prison. When you get home, your household system will have a message from me that has the contact information of a repair technician. She is one of us, Fred, a reader. You will contact this woman and make arrangements to have her repair your wall-screen, with perhaps one minor modification."

"Modification?"

"Oh yes, she knows how to add an off switch to the wall-screen power feed that will allow you to turn it off without alerting your building's internal network."

Fred blinked. "Is that possible? Why didn't I think of that?"

"It is possible, she put an off switch on my wall-screen as well, so I know it works."

"That will be glorious! No more wall-screen!"

Devon held up one hand. "Not so fast. You can't just turn it off permanently. Your neighbors will notice that, and you'll be sitting in here again before you know it. Reduce the volume in little increments, slowly over time, to acclimate the people in surrounding flats to a reduced volume of ambient sound. You'll be able to turn it off for a few hours a day at most. Do you understand?"

"Yes."

"Very good. I've purged your file. Officially, you were never here."

"Thank you, Inspector."

Devon stood. "Call me Devon. I'd like to invite you to my house next week. I have friends that I think you'll like. Readers. Writers. Thinkers. We get together regularly, lend each other books, discuss philosophy, politics and all the other things that scare the people in power. Interested?"

Fred rubbed his wrists as Devon took off the handcuffs. "Yes, definitely!"

"Excellent. I'll send you the details." He shook Fred's hand. "Until then. Mr. Pierce, you are a free man!"

* * * *

Fred made himself comfortable on his couch, a paperback book in his hands. "Silence is the perfectest herald of joy." The moment he spoke that phrase, a quote from Shakespeare, the wall-screen, the ambient music and everything else in the room fell silent. He closed his eyes and listened. He took a deep breath and exhaled through lips that wore a broad smile. The room would never be completely quiet—his neighbor's warbling wall-screens would prevent that—but with his own vidlink off it was as quiet as he could remember it being, and he rejoiced. Tonight he would attend his second discussion-group at Devon's residence. He had thoroughly enjoyed his last visit and was eager to go again tonight. That was hours away though, and until then he would read. He opened his book and read the opening line aloud. "Once upon a time and a very good time it was. . . ."

The End of Darkness

Paula Welker

His shoulders were in flames. He'd expected it—he had been on the "display wall," the prisoners' bitter nickname for the short corridor leading to the lower Rethallan sentencing chambers, countless times over the past years. Still, knowing what was coming didn't make the agony any less.

Years. Had it really been years?

His mind shied away from that enormity and he shifted, trying to take the pressure off of his shoulders by pushing with his bare toes against the slate tiling. It had been hours since he'd given up trying to gain any leverage with his wrists. They were manacled to the wall behind, but the chain offered just enough slack that he couldn't force himself up against it. It was just as well—even given the swift Elvesh healing response, his lower arms had been raw for weeks after the last time.

pushing with his feet, though, was little better. Whether Trevenorre had kept other Elvesh prisoners or whether another unfortunate had just been very tall or whether it had been installed specifically for him, the short steel bar was in exactly the wrong place—too high for him to gain much more than precarious purchase no matter how he scrabbled at the floor. His toes cramped and he stopped, slumping forward. The bar bit into his tender armpits and his shoulders exploded. He pushed up again without thinking, felt the pain in his feet, and blew out once, snatching control of himself. That managed, if barely, he settled his weight gently back onto the bar. It was too much, too automatic no matter how he tried to fight it. In three days when they came to remove him back to his cell, there would be blood from the constant scrape of his toes against the stone.

At least it distracted from the pain of his other wounds, although his questioning this time and the beating that followed had been almost perfunctory—as if they had been more interested in filling an extra spot on the wall than in any kind of answers. Or, heaven help him, as if the Rethallan king had simply been bored and required some activity to occupy his time.

King. The title had never rightfully belonged to Ransanin Trevenorre, and his actions had long since refuted any semi-legitimate claim he might once have asserted. The man had dispensed of his own family to gain the throne and then held his rule over the course of four hundred long years through terror and violence and paranoia, and any who raised a hand in protest were murdered outright or consigned to the deepest dungeons as rebels or spies. More than two years into his imprisonment, Aeshan still wasn't entirely certain that he had come out on the better end.

The long, dark days *had* given him more than adequate time to reflect on the myriad mistakes that they had made in coming to Rethalla. They had been impatient, and they had paid the price. Years of dusty, wearing travel with Huyana and Sen-deth, years of gathering every bit of post-coup memoir or suppressed Rethallan history, wasted. Years of reading and translating, of comparing notes with Darin, of sifting through the mounds of books and parchment for even the smallest hint that the whispers they had heard might be true, wasted. Their research had been exhaustive. Their plan of action had been ill-conceived and riddled with potential for disaster.

They had been idiots.

Sen-deth, of course, hadn't been allowed to participate. It was the one decent decision they had made. As the crown prince of a neighboring kingdom, the political consequences if he were caught would be disastrous. He'd not been happy about staying behind, to say the least, but he was smart, and had eventually bowed to the wisdom of Huyana's arguments. Aeshan wondered if Sen-deth knew what had happened to them—if he'd been able to glean any information at all about their fate, or if they'd simply disappeared off the face of the continent. It was an unsettling thought.

He had no idea what had happened to his friends Darin and Tak-ar, and didn't expect that he would ever know. If there was a part of their plan that had made him uneasy from the first, it was the idea of sending those two to Phaedra. He would have trusted either of them with his life, but they had too much history with the Shining

City. Darin was, for all practical purposes, banished from the country, and tall, dark Tak-ar would stick out like a sore thumb. There was simply too much chance that they would be recognized and apprehended. Still, Darin had maintained that they were the best ones to go, given their familiarity with the city and the language. Aeshan always suspected that Darin's argument was primarily based on his desire to see his homeland again rather than any of those given reasons, but he had allowed himself to be convinced. He had wanted it too badly.

He wondered if the cousins had managed to succeed in their task, or if their foray into the Shining City had ended in a dungeon as well, or worse. It was a dangerous business, going up against Ransanin Trevenorre—even in secret, even beyond the Rethallan borders. His reach was long.

Huyana, though, was the one who plagued his waking thoughts and haunted his nightmares. Huyana. His sister was intelligent and brave and loyal, and he could have chosen no one better to stand with him in such a risky endeavor. She was also beautiful, even by Elvesh standards. Outside of Elve, her delicately pointed ears, slitted pupils, honey-colored features would be considered exotic, stunning. Rethallan nobility had been known to pay nothing short of a king's ransom for an Elvesh slave. The scene flashed before his eyes again, three slavers dragging his struggling sister toward the waiting wagon as the long-knife buried itself in his lung, removing his own ability to even protest.

It had been two years. More than two years. What had become of her? He didn't want to think about it, but on most days it never left him.

He should have protected her. He should never have risked her in the first place.

He swore and jerked against the restraining bar, letting the pain swallow him. It was no more than he deserved, for sentencing them to this end. Two of the prisoners looked around, dull curiosity briefly lifting their faces. The other two had been chained to the wall for almost a full three days, and were too far gone in pain and hunger to care. He was about to repeat the gesture when the door at the far end rattled and slammed open. Light flooded in, painful against pupils that had been full blown for most of the past two years. He squeezed his eyes shut and looked away until the door closed again, leaving them in the usual sooty torchlight. He blinked, and eyed the newcomers. Someone was about to have an unpleasant day. The lower sentencing chamber only ever brought painful interrogation and either prison or death. There was no need for Trevenorre to keep up his veneer in this room, away from prying eyes—not that he bothered much with it in any situation.

He recognized the man in the lead from his years of research. Iven Janis was the son and heir of Ged Janis, one of Rethalla's Ten Barons—or possibly the Baron himself, if something had happened to his father while Aeshan had been rotting underground. Next was a soldier of some sort, and last a slave, if he read the chains and Janis's attitude correctly. Strange that Trevenorre would concern himself with the discipline of a slave. That was usually left in the hands of their masters, slaves being generally considered beneath the notice of a king.

Or, perhaps not so strange. Something about this slave caught Aeshan's eye—a calm, straight-shouldered confidence that all but dwarfed his bickering captors. This man was dangerous. Prisoner he might be, but he was no slave, regardless of what Janis and his soldier seemed to believe. Maybe, somehow, Trevenorre saw it as well.

The prisoner looked around, as though he felt Aeshan's scrutiny, and for a moment their eyes met. The shadowed brown irises flickered, swept Aeshan once before turning for a quick inspection of the other captives. He looked back to Aeshan as they passed, and the soldier swore and yanked at his chains. The prisoner stumbled, but didn't drop his gaze. His eyes conveyed grim humor and a familiarity that Aeshan didn't understand, and then the three were gone through the door into the sentencing chamber. The rasp of the sliding bolt sent his skin to crawling, as always.

He heard the other noises, too—the murmurings, the shouting, a few crashes, all muffled by the heavy door. He strained to pick out words, but from experience he knew that was pointless. One of the other prisoners eyed the inner door, too, trying to appear uninterested. The other conscious man didn't bother to look up, and the last two were likely not even aware that anyone had passed. It didn't matter. They were here as a warning to incoming captives, it wasn't necessary for them to register their surroundings. In fact, they probably served Trevenorre's purposes better that way.

The interrogation, assuming there were actually any questions being asked, didn't last as long as he would have expected. He jumped when the door crashed open, and the pain flared. He muffled his groan, but it didn't make any difference. No one was paying any attention to him.

The prisoner was, unsurprisingly, bloody. He didn't move as though he was in pain, though, or even uncomfortable. He actually appeared just short of smug, a self-satisfied grin lurking at the corners of his mouth. The soldier was expressionless, but Janis radiated a fury bordering on murderous. He stalked ahead of the other two halfway down the corridor, then turned abruptly and struck the prisoner on the face twice in quick succession. The prisoner stumbled back and tripped over the trailing chain. He landed on his knees, grunted, and squinted up at Janis. Then he turned his head, spat blood to the side, and wiped a forearm across his mouth. A taunt radiated from every line of his posture, and it took Aeshan a moment to understand.

The exposed skin was entirely uninjured.

Janis swore loudly and began to pace in tight circles. The soldier hovered uncertainly. The prisoner remained on his knees, waiting for his captors to make the next move.

A healer, then. And an impressive one, if Aeshan's admittedly limited knowledge of healers served him correctly. No trance, no trace of the original injury, almost no time involved. Huyana was the medicine man, not he, but she had shown some interest in healers in the past and he didn't remember ever hearing about such a thing from her. Maybe he had simply missed it, but with the way Janis was reacting he didn't think so. This was something out of the ordinary.

"Bury him," Janis snarled at the soldier. "I want him so drugged he can't fix a hangnail." He turned and stormed toward the outer doorway, leaving the others to follow in his wake.

For the first time, wariness flickered on the prisoner's face, and to Aeshan's surprise, the brown eyes cut briefly to him. The soldier was smirking when the prisoner looked back, and a dull red flush climbed his neck, visible even in the torchlight.

He was not, apparently, quite as confident as he made out. Anger stirred again, deep in Aeshan's gut. They had no right. Janis had no right, *Trevenorre* had no right. The soldier jerked his prisoner up and marched him out of the corridor. The door clanged shut after them, the echoes choked in the tiny corridor. The silence was heavy, smothering.

They had no *right*. Trevenorre had taken a just, prosperous kingdom, a strong ally, and turned it into a reclusive, paranoid, brutal land. He had exterminated his family in order to lay to claim his throne, and what matter if he hadn't actually killed them, as Aeshan now believed to be true? They had only told a few others about their suspicions, and their findings. Sen-deth might convince someone to take up the hunt if none of the original four returned, but that had been a difficult proposition even before. Very few of those they had trusted actually believed that the other Trevenorres might still be alive somewhere. This first failure would make his task almost impossible. And then how long before anyone else was willing to follow the clues, faint as they were, and take another run at Trevenorre? Another four hundred years? Longer? Aeshan banged his head into the wall behind him, this time in gentle despair. It was his fault. The others had been anxious as well, but the project had belonged to him from the start, and the blame belonged to him, too.

Not that blame would accomplish anything. It rarely ever did. But there was very little else to think about, here in the dark depths of Ransanin Trevenorre's prison.

Time stretched and warped, as it always did on the wall, until Aeshan wasn't certain if he'd been chained for hours or days. He couldn't trust his stomach—it was always empty. He couldn't trust the torches—the guards were sporadic about lighting and damping them, with no relation to the time of day or night. They'd been lit since he'd arrived, but they were running out of fuel, guttering. He hoped that they wouldn't go out. He had enough of complete blackness in his cell. He couldn't trust the traffic through the corridor—some days no one came through, some days two or three. He would know when they came to release him that it had been three days, but until then time remained a slippery thing.

The rasp of the inner chamber bolt jerked him awake. That sound would have roused him from any depth of sleep. He peered dumbly around, squinting for a glimpse of whoever had passed. One of the torches had gone out, three clung tenaciously to life, but he saw nothing, heard nothing. Even the narrow strip of light that usually filtered beneath the chamber door while occupied seemed to be missing. He squeezed his eyes shut, not certain the mystery was worth the effort. He was still trying to decide when the faintest groan of hinges reached his ears—again from the inner door, not the outer. Aeshan squinted against the dancing light and his headache, and just made out a solitary figure slipping from the chamber into the display corridor.

It had never happened before, a single person leaving the sentencing chamber in the dark. For one wild moment he expected Trevenorre himself to materialize in the dim torchlight, the only man who never entered or left the chamber through the corridor. Then the near torch threw its faltering light onto the frayed brown curls and lean frame of Janis's healer. His mind went blank, and he swore aloud, unaware of what invectives he even managed to produce. The healer looked toward him and motioned for silence, then surveyed the others and moved swiftly to the semi-conscious man just inside the inner door.

The healer seized the man's shoulder where the rough cotton tunic met battered skin, and before the exhausted prisoner could even look up or understand what was happening, he was asleep. The healer stayed for a moment, eyes narrowed in concentration, then moved on to the next man, sunk into unconsciousness across the corridor from Aeshan. He gripped that man's shoulder as well, and in a few brief moments the labored breathing quieted to a slow, deep rhythm. Aeshan watched with awe as the healer moved on to the next man, marveling not only at the speed but at the very fact of what he was witnessing. Why bother with this? If the man had escaped and was on the run, it was an insane waste of time. The other, more wistful part of his mind was busy pondering how nice it would be if Elve, unlike other humans, weren't immune to healer's energy. It was true that his own body would take care of itself swiftly enough, but at the moment he could think of nothing better than a hand on his shoulder and a swift release from pain.

Nothing was ever that easy.

The healer finished the last two in quick succession, and strode across the tiles to Aeshan. Before Aeshan could tell him not to bother, the healer was fumbling with the wrist manacles.

"Aeshan Saquya?"

For a moment, he was too shocked to respond. He hadn't heard his name in over two years—he'd made a point not to give it to Trevenorre or any of his squadron of torturers. It had been a costly business, that, but he'd never regretted it. And now this complete stranger spoke as though he were simply making an acquaintance at some party they were both reluctant to attend. He eyed the healer again. He was Rethallan. Could he be trusted? Perhaps it was all a trick of some sort.

"What makes you think that?"

The healer looked up and grinned, unoffended. "You look a lot like your sister." He gave one final yank on the manacles, which fell open with a muffled clatter of steel against stone. The healer crouched to work on his ankles, and Aeshan gaped.

"How do you—"

The healer pursed his lips together and shook his head. It was all Aeshan could do to obey, but the ankle cuffs had come open, leaving him free of the wall. The healer stood, tucking a short steel sliver that Aeshan recognized as a pared-down knitting needle into his waistband, and took his arm. Gently he eased Aeshan's burning shoulders around and away from the bar, and for a moment blackness that had nothing to do with a badly-lit corridor tinged his vision. The healer supported him until he could prop himself against the wall, shaking from the pain in his shoulders and from a dozen other wounds flared to life. When he finally opened his eyes again, the healer was eyeing the outer door nervously.

"We need to go. Are you well?"

No, but he was well enough. He nodded.

"Good." The healer hesitated, glanced again toward the far doorway, and then held out his hand, palm up. "Jase."

The gesture was so familiar, so uniquely Elvesh, that it took his breath away, and for a moment Aeshan was forced to close his eyes again. Then, he slapped his own hand down firmly, gripping the healer's wrist and feeling long fingers close over his own battered skin. It was a greeting usually reserved for family and close friends, but he supposed that breaking him out of prison made this Jase the first friend he'd had in a very long time.

They broke contact quickly, and Jase moved to pull Aeshan's arm over his shoulder. He was tall enough to actually be helpful, and he locked an arm firmly around Aeshan's waist. The first wavering step almost resulted in disaster, and Aeshan swore again, softly. It was a bad habit he'd picked up in prison, with nothing but screams and curses making up the entirety of the spoken noise around him. Jase shook his head. "Don't waste your breath. And, we're not going that way." He guided Aeshan away from the outer door, back toward the sentencing chamber. Aeshan stiffened, but Jase gripped his wrist and picked up their pace. "It's all right, it's safer than going out into the general corridors."

True. Aeshan nodded, ashamed to be caught in his fear, and forced himself to keep up. Jase pulled them both through the doorway and lowered Aeshan to the floor, then heaved the door shut and shot the bolt. Aeshan shivered, reflexively. A spark struck. Jase kindled a tiny torch and propped it between them.

"Miserable place, I know, sorry, but at least we can't see most of it."

That was also true, though not as much for him as it would be for Jase. He nodded, and returned to the subject burning a hole in his mind. "You know my sister?"

Jase settled onto the tiles, body still coiled for a quick strike, if necessary. "For more than two years now." He eyed Aeshan. "She saw you stabbed, she thinks you're dead."

He blew out a long breath. It was a pain he'd known only too well these past years, believing the worst about someone he loved. "Huyana, though? She's safe?"

"She is." Jase's eyes hardened. His lifted eyebrow conveyed a wealth of meaning. "And unharmed."

It was almost more than he could handle. He rested his forehead on his knees and offered every short prayer of thanksgiving he knew in rapid succession. Then he nodded. "Thank you." He gazed around the darkened room, careful not to focus on any one thing. His eyes were better than the average human's. Their small torch was more than enough light for him, and he had no desire to see any particulars here. "If she thinks I'm dead, I guess you're not here after me, then." His attempt at levity was rewarded with an amused snort.

"Not quite. I'm not here on purpose for any reason, unfortunately. And it was a complete accident I saw you on the way through, Janis had no plans to let me anywhere near Trevenorre." He held up his hands, and Aeshan saw branding scars, old ones, marked into his palms. "He's got a score to settle. I guess he hoped to, uh, extract the information himself, once he got his hands on me again, but Trevenorre gave him very little choice."

If he wasn't a slave now, he had been at some point. And to Janis himself, apparently. Aeshan would have wondered about the man's story, if his own wasn't currently so desperate.

"What information is that?"

Jase hesitated, then offered an odd half-grin. "He wants to know what Kethaloren and Esharla Trevenorre are planning."

For a moment, his mind refused to process that statement. The words chased each other individually, declining to string themselves into any coherent meaning, beating against the insides of his aching skull. After a frantic moment, the chaos subsided for long enough for him to whisper, "*What?*"

"You were right. They were there." Jase's voice lowered, too—gentle, clipped, hurried. "We found Kethaloren Trevenorre in the catacombs beneath St. John's in Yesh. Esharla was in Phaedra, sealed into an ancient archive under the Central Library." He gripped Aeshan's shoulder. "They're alive. You were right."

The entire world crashed in on him. He'd been *right,* all this time. All the years of travel, all the years of research and planning, all the years of *prison—not* wasted. He couldn't breathe.

"And they'll help defeat him?"

"They already are. They've been at it since we woke them." *Woke them?* Now wasn't the time for that kind of detail, although he was dying to know how Trevenorre had managed to suppress the rest of his family so completely for all of these years. "Khar-an and Elve are onboard, of course, and Sul Mare. Also a group of Rethallans living in Pral. They don't all have the purist of motives, but Kethaloren seems to think he can handle them. We're having some trouble with the Pralian government, and Trevelan won't give us a firm answer. We didn't even bother with Canth, they're too tight with Trevenorre. Hopefully, we won't need any of them anyway—Kethaloren and Esharla have been trying to find a way to do this without starting a war, but it's best to be prepared for that regardless." Jase shook his head. "This is Ransanin Trevenorre we're talking about."

It was too much to take in at once—his head was spinning, and not just from the news. It had been entirely too long since he'd eaten. Jase's hand tightened on his shoulder.

"We need to get going. They'll find me gone before long, if they haven't already. Hold still."

Before he could question the contradictory statements, a prickling sensation spread throughout his body, ending in a rush of energy that left his skin tingling and the edges of his vision sparkling. Jase removed his hand, and Aeshan rotated his shoulder, staring. It no longer hurt. In fact, nothing hurt—not his ribs, not his head, not his face or feet or. . . .

"That's impossible." He rose abruptly, relishing the lack of pain, gaping at the smooth, faintly scarred skin around his wrists. "Elve are immune to healers."

Jase stood, too, gathering their small torch and his flint. "That's exactly what Huyana said, the first time. I had no idea it wasn't supposed to work, which I guess is good because I probably never would have even tried it otherwise. Neither of us knew what to make of it, but when we learned my father was Elvesh, she seemed to think that explained it." He grinned faintly. "I've found that she's right more often than not about those kinds of things."

Aeshan was distracted from the rarity of a true half-Elvesh by the familiarity with which Jase spoke of his sister. He paced behind the healer to the far end of the room.

"You know Huyana well, then?"

"Aye." Jase handed back the torch and felt beneath the edges of the room's only tapestry, a ragged, ghastly affair that had always seemed entirely out of place beside the room's other contents. Aeshan pushed back a surge of frustration.

"And you see her often?"

Jase stopped his search and stood still for a moment, then sighed and turned back to Aeshan. His expression was cautious. "As often as any man sees his wife, I suppose."

"*Wife?*" The word exploded out of him before he could stop it. "No. Elve don't marry other. . . ."

"Didn't you just finish telling me that Elve were immune to healers, too?" Jase set his jaw and shook his head. "Sorry, but it's not a lie." He dug beneath the neckline of his tunic and freed a battered, red-stained leather band threaded through a long, carved, dark green jade.

An Elvesh wedding stone.

At Jase's nod, Aeshan stepped closer and took it between his fingers. He held the torch close and studied the finely carved Elvesh symbols which declared the binding of Huyana Saquya to Jase of Rethalla, by Elvesh priest in the palace at Zar-en. The design and etchings were flawless, wrought by a craftsman who was no less than a master in his trade.

His sister had married, and he had missed it.

Aeshan dropped the stone and stepped back, rubbing at his head. Jase—his brother-in-law, they were family—spoke before he could form any words.

"I realize how unusual it is." Unusual was one word for it. Exceedingly rare would have been a closer fit. "I know that half of her lifetime will be left when I die. I know that she'll have to raise any children we might have alone, for the most part. I made sure she thought about that, too." Jase's eyes locked with his own. "I wouldn't have allowed her to make this commitment lightly, not knowing what she'll eventually go through." Aeshan offered a careful nod. Jase sighed, and looked away. "But, we looked hell in the eyes together and saved each other from it. It wasn't . . . it's not something that . . . I knew I'd never look at another woman again, but I would never have put myself forward to her, not as things stood." He laughed softly. "I guess she got tired of waiting. She gave me two hours to get ready and back to the chapel after she proposed. I almost couldn't get my witness there in time."

Huyana had proposed? Aeshan actually laughed out loud, startled that he remembered how. "Yes. That's definitely my sister you married." He hesitated, then held out his hand again, steadier now that he understood. "If you should be blessed with children, she won't raise them alone."

Jase's head snapped up, and a relieved grin flashed across his tired features. He seized Aeshan's arm. "Thank you."

Aeshan nodded, once, and released him. "Now. What are we doing here? I assume that since you found a way in, you can get us back out?" He eyed the dark corners of the room, unease returning. "I'm ready to be done with this place."

"Agreed." Jase turned back to the tapestry and shoved the heavy material aside. Dust coated the air. A faded wooden doorframe stood out against the stone. "The King's Halls. Tevlar Trevenorre's grandfather had an entire system of back halls built into the palace, which only the royal family were permitted to use. Apparently he found it faster to get around when he didn't have to stop and be polite every three feet or so." His faint grin reappeared. "Esharla accuses him of being antisocial, but that's a bit of a pot-kettle accusation. She and Kethaloren have quite the affinity for secret passages themselves. From what I've seen, the entire family is fond of the concept of as many back doors as possible."

"I've always wondered how he gets in and out." Aeshan inspected the beaten wood, ignoring the ease with which Jase spoke of the royal family. For a former slave, he appeared to be well-stocked with companions of significance. At least he wasn't about to find out that the man had married Esharla Trevenorre . . . "I assumed it must be something like."

Jase twitched the brittle handle and nudged the door open. "I don't think they were actually much of a secret in Tevlar's time, I'd imagine that all of this hiding doorways came along with Ransanin. I had a terrible time finding an entrance."

"I don't imagine he fancies much of anyone knowing there's an entire system of corridors in the palace where he can be found alone and unguarded."

"Right."

Aeshan snugged the door closed and squinted down the long, low hall. "What if we run across him in here?"

"In here?" Jase seemed startled by the thought. He chewed on his lip, and shook his head. "Let's hope we don't. I'd rather not take the chance that we can subdue him in these quarters without anyone hearing." He patted the dusty stone. "I doubt these inner walls are that thick."

Subdue, not kill. That would indeed be best, he supposed—and for more reasons than one. Aeshan made a mental note to stay vigilant. *If* they did meet Trevenorre in these corridors, their best defense would plenty of warning. "Do you know how we get out? Do these passages go all the way to the outside?"

Jase pushed away from the wall and started down the hall. "We can't leave just yet, we've got another stop to make."

"*What?*" Aeshan hurried after him, ducking so that his head didn't scrape the low ceiling. "What are you playing at? In case you hadn't noticed, we're completely outnumbered. You said yourself that it was only a matter of time before they—"

"The king is here," Jase hissed, swinging around.

The obviousness of that statement baffled him, until he suddenly realized that Jase had never referred to Ransanin Trevenorre by that title. Which meant. . . .

"Tevlar Trevenorre is *here*?" Adrenaline surged, leaving him lightheaded and shivering. Despite the extra energy Jase had provided, his starved limbs wouldn't support him through this level of activity for much longer. He really had to find something to eat.

Jase nodded, and resumed his stride. "In the old chapel."

Unfortunately, that just wasn't going to happen any time soon. In any case, he'd give up another week's worth of meals to help free Tevlar Trevenorre, to see the result of all of his efforts standing before him in the flesh. He crossed his arms and tucked his hands beneath to hide the tremors. "How do you know? We never found anything about—"

"Trevenorre gave himself away." Jase shook his head. "He was trying to intimidate me, I was barely listening, and then there it was. Not in so many words, but when I finally realized what he had said . . . " He halted at an intersection, peered into two dark openings, then kept straight. "There wasn't much else it could mean."

Aeshan gripped the torch. "It's a big risk to take for something you heard 'not in so many words.'"

Jase cast a shallow grin over his shoulder. "You can stay here if you want."

"Don't be stupid."

The grin widened. "It might be fun, you know. See the palace, save the kingdom."

Huyana's husband was apparently insane. "What if he let it slip on purpose?"

"I thought of that." Jase sobered. "It's a big mistake, for a man so guarded. It's possible, and worth keeping an eye out, but I don't believe it. He had no reason to, and every reason to be cautious. His brother and sister are the biggest real threat he's faced in four hundred years, there's no way he would risk freeing his father as well, not on purpose. I think he's starting to get rattled, finally—and about time. Anyway, you know how Trevenorre works. He prefers brute force. That cat and mouse kind of thing isn't really in his repertoire."

That was true enough. His new brother-in-law had a good grasp of political motivation. "All right. Do you know how to get there?"

"Well . . . " Jase halted at another intersection and studied it, then kept on straight again. "I saw something that I think was the entrance to the old chapel when they were dragging me down here earlier. It was locked off with a steel lattice and the inner corridor walls were all mosaic, which sounds like what Kethaloren described. So, if we go up a flight and keep headed in that direction, I'm hoping we'll run across it. We might have to stick our heads out of a few doors now and then to be sure we stay on the right course."

"Fabulous."

"Glad you like it. Huyana would have called me an idiot."

"Right, but . . . some things don't need to be said out loud."

"Exactly my thought as well."

Insane he might be, but Aeshan liked the man.

In the end, they didn't need to look out of any doors to keep their bearings. When they reached the ground level, they found that some ambitious former family member had marked each of the doors set into the dark hallway in flowing calligraphy, detailing the room or set of rooms beyond.

"Probably one of the ladies." Aeshan ran his fingers over the fading words above one door. Formal Dining Room. The hinges were thick with rust—it seemed that Trevenorre had no use for this particular exit. "At least, I'm quite sure I would have given up after the first few and just memorized the exits."

"I'm glad for it, whoever's responsible." Jase squinted down the hall. "I think we're going the wrong way again. I didn't see anything that looked like a dining room when they brought me through, I'm beginning to think we turned the wrong way at the entrance hall."

"I'm surprised they took you through any of the main section. It's not really done, dragging prisoners through formal areas where the sensibilities of ladies and children might be disturbed. I never saw anything but underground and back corridors."

Jase snorted softly. "I'm an associate of Kethaloren and Esharla Trevenorre. Trevenorre doesn't want his people, any of them, left in any doubt what happens to those who openly oppose him."

He didn't have anything to say to that, so he kept his mouth shut and followed Jase back down the hall. Three quarters and two more wrong turns later, they finally stood before a low door marked "Chapel." Aeshan took a deep breath, and looked at Jase. The healer rubbed his hands together nervously.

"Problem?"

Jase shook his head. "No. I only hope I'm right about this."

"That the king is here, or that Trevenorre wasn't leading you into a trap?"

"Both."

"Amen, then. And I hope that this doesn't turn into the shortest prison break in Rethallan history."

"Right." Jase closed his eyes for a moment, whispering beneath his breath, and Aeshan recognized the words of an ancient Elvesh prayer. For a Rethallan, his brother-in-law spoke Elvesh exceptionally well. Before Aeshan could add his own silent plea, Jase grasped the tarnished handle and pulled.

The door shuddered, but remained closed. Jase swore softly. “Locked.”

“Did you expect otherwise? If his father really is here, Trevenorre would be a complete fool to leave it open for just anyone who happens to stumble along.”

“I was hoping.” Jase removed his homemade lock-pick from his waistband and knelt, peering into the lock. “It’s rusty in there, I hope this works.” He slid the slender instrument into the lock and began to gently work at the inner mechanism.

“Well, Trevenorre’s not known for his piety, is he?” Aeshan peered back down the hall, alert for any movement or sound that might indicate they were not alone. They’d heard no hint of company to this point, but it was only a matter of time before Janis or his soldier found Jase missing and flooded the palace with guards in the search—if they hadn’t already. “He probably hasn’t used this door since he locked the king away.”

“Maybe.” Jase shifted his position and tried again. Aeshan fell silent, waiting, and was beginning to think that they would be forced to try to kick the door down when a rusty snick reached his ears. “We’re in.” Jase tucked the lock-pick back into his belt and pulled at the door. It didn’t move. Jase fell to swearing, and Aeshan pushed him aside. Even half-starved, Elve were stronger than any other humans on the continent.

The Khar-an might argue with that, and probably would—but there were no Khar-an present at the moment, so that entire point was moot. He shook his head. His mind was wandering. Or, perhaps he was a little insane himself. At this point, it was a bit difficult to decide.

"Look at the hinges. This isn't going anywhere without help." He turned the handle and yanked on the door, and twice more when it didn't budge. It finally flew open in a shower of rust, and Aeshan stumbled back, bracing himself before he hit the opposite wall. Jase stepped by him.

"Thanks. You're useful, you Elve."

"Good to know." Aeshan brushed away the rusty flakes from his fingers and clothes, and followed Jase into the chapel.

The first thing he noticed was the light. It was dim, filtering through stained glass dark with years of accumulated dust, dirt, and pollen, but still a good sight preferable to the pitch black of the King's Halls. The air tasted heavy, unused—dry and musty, still and warm. It pressed on his lungs, and he dragged in a deep breath, surveying the wreck of what had been the Trevenorre family chapel.

It might have been beautiful once, but that time was long past. Besides the grimy windows and the thick layer of dust over every other surface in the room, most of the furniture lay shattered in heaps against the walls. The room had not just been abandoned—it had been deliberately wrecked. Heavy wooden chairs were reduced to little better than kindling. Candles lay in the cracks between the floor tiles, half-melted from the heat of long years. Vases lay in chalky pieces near the altar, the decayed remnants of their last contents scattered across the stone surface. The altar and the tabernacle alone remained untouched, and Aeshan was relieved to see, in a glance through the open door, that the tabernacle was empty. Beside him, Jase shook his head and moved away from the door.

"I wonder if this happened during the coup, or . . . after."

After? If Trevenorre had done this himself, he meant. Aeshan didn't want to think about it. He had given up trying to fathom Ransanin Trevenorre's mind long ago.

"I'm guessing he didn't accidentally say where *exactly* he put the king."

"He did not." Jase shrugged, and moved to the far wall. "Start looking. Anything that could be a trapdoor or a hidden recess or . . . well, I don't know."

"I'll use my imagination."

They split apart, and for the better part of two quarters Aeshan inspected every crevice, every crack, every loose tile in the rear portion of the chapel. He was beginning to think that Trevenorre truly had lied, or that Jase had misunderstood, or that they were somehow in the wrong chapel, or that, for any number of other reasons, they were either going to have to leave empty-handed or end up back in chains—because there was no prayer that Janis's soldier hadn't discovered Jase missing by now, and the corridor guard might have even noticed his own absence as well—when Jase hissed sharply from beneath the window. He abandoned the back wall and bolted across the tiny space.

"Did you find something?"

"I think so. Help me here."

Jase was clearing debris away from a section of flooring. Aeshan joined him, noting that the tiles beneath seemed lighter than their surrounding neighbors. He squinted at the wood and marble spread around them.

"Some kind of cabinet, I guess?" He frowned, trying to understand what Jase had seen. "I don't. . . ."

"Look." Jase pointed to a hole the size of his forefinger bored into one of the lighter tiles. At first Aeshan thought it might nothing more than a bolt-hole, where the cabinet had been secured to the floor, but closer inspection showed that the hole continued through the stone, beyond his ability to see its end. "And here, and here." Jase pointed out several more in rapid succession, forming a rectangular area around the window. "Air holes. They have to breath, he couldn't completely seal them away." Aeshan helped him heave the last bit of lumber away from the wall, leaving a wide clear spot beneath the window. "I'm an idiot, I should have thought of it before. Both of the others were—"

"I wouldn't worry about it." Aeshan slid a finger into one of the holes. "We've got . . . " He stopped, surprised. "These aren't even very thick, I can feel a space down beneath." He gripped another one of the air holes, and tugged experimentally on the tile. "It's not heavy, either. Just a matter of getting . . . Here." He nodded for Jase to work free the rest of the tile. Together they managed to pry it away and toss it aside. With the first gone the others came quickly, and in a matter of moments they were staring into a long, shallow pit dug into the chapel foundation.

The figure inside might have been dead but for the shallow rise and fall of his chest. He might have been only asleep, but for the utter stillness of every other muscle, the utter absence of sound, the complete lack of response to their crashing around above him. In the torchlight Aeshan could just make out a shaggy beard and heavy, out-of-date attire. His breath fled him, and he sat down, hard, where he was.

Tevlar Trevenorre was alive. He was alive, and they had found him.

They had found him.

"Aeshan, breathe." Jase's words jerked him back to the present. He sucked a deep breath, and swiped his forearm across his suddenly wet eyes. Jase was already inside the hole, and Aeshan scrambled to help him haul the king up and around the support beams. They laid him out on the chapel floor. "All right." Jase knelt at his head. "I need you hold him down."

"What?"

"They're in the middle of a coup, as far as they know. The other two were violent coming out of it, I'm not looking for another concussion."

Ah. Aeshan placed a hand on each of Tevlar Trevenorre's shoulders, and a knee in his abdomen for good measure. That done, he nodded to Jase and sucked in a breath, waiting.

"Aeshan. Breathe."

He coughed out a laugh. "Right."

"Right." Jase grinned and closed his eyes. Apparently, whatever needed done was complex enough that it actually required him to trance. Aeshan would be interested to learn more about his brother-in-law's odd healing abilities, when time and leisure permitted.

Seconds passed, and the silence wrapped around him, soothing him, strangling him. . . .

And then Tevlar Trevenorre convulsed, and rocked forward, and it was all that Aeshan could do to keep him pinned down. The king twisted beneath him and kicked out, and Aeshan dug in with his knee, drawing a gasp and a snarl. He tightened his grip on Trevenorre's shoulder, and threw his weight down when the man tried to roll away. Trevenorre slammed a knee into his inner thigh, and Aeshan swore roundly.

Beneath him, Trevenorre paused.

"Your Majesty, we're friends!" He barked the words out, gasping around the pain in his leg. Jase seized the opportunity to pin down Trevenorre's legs.

"Your Majesty—"

Trevenorre retaliated, nearly throwing them both. An elbow slammed into Aeshan's mouth, and around the pain he barely heard Jase panting, "Your Majesty! The fish in Olifusen taste better than the deer in Canth!"

The words were gibberish, but Tevlar Trevenorre fell suddenly still beneath them. For a long moment no one moved, and Aeshan risked a glance at the king. The dark blue eyes were locked on Jase, who slowly lifted himself off of Trevenorre's legs.

"Your Majesty—"

"Where did you hear that?" The king's voice was hoarse, as though centuries of disuse had left his vocal chords uncertain of their function. Jase sat back. Trevenorre's voice sharpened. "Where did you—"

"Koren, your Majesty. He gave me the passcode in case I should ever have need of it."

The name was completely unfamiliar to him, but not to Trevenorre. The king mouthed it silently, eyes still pinning Jase, then barked, "And what response were you to receive?"

Jase snorted. "That Olifusen's fish might taste better, but Saichel's bear are more challenging."

It was the most ridiculous passcode Aeshan had ever heard, but it brought the desired results. Trevenorre studied Jase for another long moment, then speared Aeshan with a glance, and finally rested his head back against the tiles. "Who are you?"

"Jase, your Majesty, in Prince Kethaloren and Lady Esharla's service." He nodded toward Aeshan. "This is Aeshan Saquya. It's largely thanks to him that we were able to locate and restore you."

Aeshan inclined his head, feeling slightly lightheaded as the unreality of the situation settled in. He was sitting on the floor of a destroyed chapel in Ransanin Trevenorre's palace in the center of Rethalla's capital, speaking to a king thought dead for more than four hundred years. . . .

"There were others involved as well, your Majesty."

Of course, it was also entirely possible that the dizziness could be mostly blamed on his almost desperate need for water and some type of sustenance.

"Restore? What do you . . . " Trevenorre's voice trailed, as his eyes began to move over their surroundings—the dusty beams, the filthy window, the broken furniture. His body tensed again. "My son!" He struggled to sit, and his voice lowered to a growl. "*Ransanin.* Where is he? What's the situation in the city? Why are we—"

"Forgive me, your Majesty. I'll explain, but we have very little time." Jase held out a hand to help the king rise, glancing behind them to the door which led back into the King's Halls. Trevenorre's eyes narrowed at the interruption, then fell on the hand before him. They riveted on the scars branded deep into Jase's palm, and snapped back to his face. Jase shook his hand, impatient, and after another long moment, Trevenorre grasped it. Jase hauled them both to their feet, then stepped back.

"Your Majesty, the situation is this. The city and Rethalla itself were lost. You and your younger children were declared dead. Ransanin executed all within the city who openly opposed him—including the foreign delegates present for your anniversary celebration. Allied ties with Elve, Khar-an, and Sul Mare were broken. What was left of the resistance grouped on the Pralian peninsula, which was finally lost to Rethalla. Your son divided the kingdom into ten baronies and appointed his supporters to administrate them. The kingdom remains in his rule to this day." He paused, drawing a deep breath. "It has been four hundred years, your Majesty. Much has changed since you last set foot outside this chapel."

Trevenorre's expression had hardened well before Jase finished speaking. He shook his head and stepped away, the hint of a sneer painting his face. "Is this idiocy the best my son can do? Does he think to trick me? To confuse me? I'm not so—"

"It's not, your Majesty." Aeshan gulped back the thought that he had just interrupted a king and plunged ahead. Janis's guards or Trevenorre's soldiers could be upon them at any time. "Years of my life have been spent travelling the continent in search of any scrap of real, uncensored history from the time after your son took the throne. A small handful of us have sifted through entire mountains of hearsay and old rubbish almost to the point of blindness for any clue of what Ransanin may have done with you and your other children if he had not, in fact, killed you. Many of my friends and family have thought me obsessed, or mad, and yet I kept on, and for my trouble I have spent two years locked away in your son's prisons. I saw my sister taken by slavers, and I have only just learned today that she is safe and unharmed. The man who is her husband," he gestured wildly to Jase, not caring that he was beginning to sound nearly as mad as some of his cousins had attempted to claim, "has lived as the property of another under your son's rule. Thousands of lives have been corrupted and destroyed over the past four hundred years, so do not say that this is idiocy." He shook his head, breathing hard, ignoring the shocked slant of Jase's eyebrow and Trevenorre's clenched jaw. "No, it is most certainly not." He fell silent, and for a long moment none of them did anything but stare. Finally, Aeshan flung his hand toward the window. "Look at this chapel! Does it seem as if it has been empty and destroyed for only a few days? Look at the hole that we took you from! Do the chisel marks seem fresh? Feel your beard! Does it seem no more than a few—"

"Stop." Tevlar Trevenorre's voice was soft, but the sheer authority conveyed in one small word brought Aeshan's rant to an abrupt halt. The king eyed him briefly, rubbing at the ragged beard, taking in Aeshan's filthy attire and likely his odor of half-rancid food and stale sweat. The blue eyes flickered to Jase, landing on his hands even though the brands were now hidden, and moved on to the ancient, dusty material that hung from his own body. He fiddled with the rotting golden piping at his wrists, looked to the uncovered hole beneath the nearly opaque stained-glass, took in the rest of the chapel with a quick, scouring gaze. Even in the dim lighting,

Aeshan saw the king's eyes begin to hollow, his face take on a gray cast. Aeshan exchanged a quick glance with Jase and stepped forward again.

"I apologize, your Majesty, but—"

Trevenorre silenced him with an abrupt shake of his head. Instead, his eyes pinned Jase. "You say Esharla and Kethaloren have been found?"

"Aye, your Majesty." Jase nodded and crossed his arms. "Kethaloren nearly two years past, your daughter in the time since."

The king was still, raking Jase with a glare that Aeshan was grateful wasn't fixed upon him. "Keselan?"

Jase shook his head. "No sign, your Majesty. And until today . . . " He glanced toward the window, mottled with flecks of light where the debris covering the glass was not solid. "Or yesterday, perhaps, we also had no idea of your whereabouts." He shifted. "Your Majesty, there is much to say but we cannot stay here long enough to say it. I've been a prisoner of one of your son's Barons these past weeks, and he'll know I'm missing by now. Aeshan's absence has surely been noted as well. We haven't—"

"*My channelers assure me that your signature remains within the palace, healer, so I trust you're listening now.*"

The familiar voice echoed around them, off of the walls and the ceiling, and before Aeshan knew he had moved he was crouched near a wall gripping a broken chair leg. He flushed, embarrassed, but neither Trevenorre nor Jase seemed to have noticed. The king began a circular pace, head tilted, eyes narrowed. Jase remained still, and Aeshan saw the sudden tension radiating from his brother-in-law's posture. He stood, gingerly, and made his way to Jase.

"What is this? How can he—"

"Channeler." Jase's voice was strained. "The whole palace can probably—"

"*Once again, you've proven your intelligence vastly superior to that of my Baron and his staff. I see why my siblings so highly value your service. I really am amazed that Janis ever managed to retain your property rights for nearly a decade—it seems the man is utterly incapable of anything more than superficial observation and shallow thought.*"

Property rights. It was appalling, such casual reference to another man as simple *property*. Jase rubbed his palms together, slowly, and stepped away from Aeshan. Aeshan cast a quick glance around the chapel. It was unnerving, this voice that came from nowhere and yet seemed to be everywhere at once. "Can he . . . hear us?" There were very few channelers left, and he knew even less about their skills than he knew about healers. Jase seemed disinclined to answer, but the king shook his head.

"Unlikely. My daughter claims it much simpler to throw a voice than to pick up voices from another location."

Esharla Trevenorre had been—*was*—a channeler of some skill. It made good sense that her father would be more than familiar with such details.

"*I would renew my previous offer, but you've made your loyalties perfectly clear and I won't waste our time. I can't say that I'm surprised—my brother was always very careful about his friends.*"

Tevlar Trevenorre halted his pacing, his gaze pinned firmly on Jase.

"*I have another offer, but it would be best if you knew the entire situation before making any decisions.*"

The entire . . . ? A woman's scream rebounded from the walls, scratching at Aeshan's eardrums, vibrating in the space around them. It cut off, and then rose again, a shriek of pain and rage. Jase froze, and the blood rushed out of his face. He was halfway to the door before it had died away.

"What—"

"Lurissa!" His voice was a strangled mix of horror and fury and . . . defeat. Aeshan started after him, but Trevenorre beat him to the door. The king seized Jase's wrist and pulled him around.

"Who is this woman?"

Jase jerked away. "Lurissa Janis."

Aeshan stared. "The Baron's—"

"Yes, the Baron's wife! It was arranged, she's hardly more to Janis than property as well, but she's a good, brave girl and she's been through a lot with us. Huyana and Koren and I went back for—"

"*So, now that you understand what's at stake, here are my terms.*" Jase stilled. "*You will return yourself into my custody in the main hall, within two quarters' time. If you do so, I will remove the Lady Janis from her husband's influence. She will remain here in the palace, unharmed and under my protection.*"

What was the word of Ransanin Trevenorre? It could hardly be trusted, any more than. . . .

"*No*!" The female voice was young and fierce. "*Don't you dare! Jase, don't you—*"

It cut off sharply, Trevenorre's voice overriding the Lady's. "*If you do not return within two quarters, my channelers will be forced to track you down. It will be a long process, but I assure you it can be done. Your own association with my sister will have shown you what a determined channeler can accomplish, I'm sure. And in the meanwhile, I will be forced to attempt to retrieve the necessary information from the Lady Janis.*

"*It's your choice, healer. Two quarters.*"

The air stilled and fell heavy on them again. Ransanin Trevenorre had finished with his ultimatum—and what an ultimatum it was.

For a long moment no one moved. Aeshan eyed his companions, wondering around his ever growing headache what to do next. What options did they possibly have? Jase's face was utterly devoid of expression, and Trevenorre's coloring had faded to a sickly gray. He was casting about for something to break the silence when Jase clasped his hands behind his head and bent over, muttering fiercely, then stood again, rubbing briskly at his face.

"I thought . . . " He blew out a long breath. "Janis found us, somehow. Not that we were particularly hiding, but . . . " He shook his head. "We'd gone out that morning, Huyana and Lurissa and I, we'd, uh, taken to walking Darin's running course in the mornings."

Aeshan nodded, his mind racing. Darin was an avid runner and his preferred course stretched for miles across the flat plain surrounding Zar-en, but in the scheme of things, it meant that Iven Janis's people had still been dangerously close to the Khar-an capital.

"They caught us off guard, Lurissa was taken. I sent Huyana back for help and went after them. I caught up and managed to free her during the night hours, but they saw us and we were forced to run. I staged a distraction and sent her the other way, I thought she'd made it . . . " He clenched his hands behind his neck again and fell back into the barely audible mutterings that Aeshan was certain didn't bear repeating.

Trevenorre eyed him. "We don't have much time, and there aren't—"

"No." Jase opened his eyes and lowered his arms, and Aeshan's gut twisted. He didn't like the sudden resolve in the healer's posture, his brisk tone. "No. We don't, and the two of you need to take advantage where you can. Your Majesty, you know the palace the best, even having been away for so long. Take the safest way out, the least likely to—"

"Jase!" Aeshan seized his arm. "What are you doing? You can't—"

"You get him out of here!" Jase snarled, turning on him. "You get him *out* of here. He's the king, he means more to—"

"Jase, stop." Trevenorre's soft voice cut through Jase's words. "We have a few minutes, just wait. It's not—"

"Not what? Not necessary? Not over? You know that's not true, your Majesty." Jase shook his head, circling for the door that would lead him back into the King's Halls. "We have nothing, it's three of us against an entire city, on Trevenorre's ground. Aeshan's dehydrated and half-starved, you're four hundred years out of date, they know I'm here. We might make it, the three of us, but without Lurissa . . . " He pounded a fist against the dark wall. "He *knows* I'm still here, he has a good idea that I won't leave without her, he'll find me eventually and you can't be with me when he does. If we can keep him in the dark, keep it from him that we found you . . . That's the best we can hope for from this. Tell me you see any other way."

Tevlar Trevenorre shook his head. "We haven't had a chance to—"

"We won't get a chance, your Majesty! We have two quarters! Less now, and I still have to get there." King and healer locked eyes for a long moment. "Your Majesty, it's imperative that you escape alive. It's a part of your duty to allow others to sacrifice for you."

If possible, Trevenorre's face blanched even further. When he spoke, his voice was a whisper. "You have my apologies, for what they're worth."

Jase snorted. "This isn't your doing."

Trevenorre straightened, his eyes hardening. "He's my son. I didn't know, I didn't even suspect, but you have my apologies nonetheless."

Jase breathed deeply. "My thanks, your Majesty." He turned to Aeshan. "I'm glad I—"

"You know he'll kill you." Aeshan could see Jase clench his jaw. "Whatever you did the last time, however you escaped, they won't leave that open again. They'll drug you, and they'll eventually kill you." He felt the anger surging from deep in his gut, where he had kept it buried deep for two long years. "Jase—"

"I can't leave her in danger. It would be like abandoning my sister to him," Jase whispered, holding out his hand. Aeshan gritted his teeth against the rant that was attempting to work its way free and gripped his brother-in-law's wrist tightly.

"And what will I tell my sister?"

Jase closed his eyes. He blew out another long breath, and dug the wedding stone out from beneath his collar. "Tell her that I love her." He snapped the leather band with a quick twist, and pressed the jade into Aeshan's hand. "And tell her that until I met her I didn't know I was even allowed to dream." He gripped Aeshan's arm, then turned back to Trevenorre. "Your Majesty, please tell Koren . . . " He stopped, and rubbed at his jaw, and laughed suddenly, the sound out of place in the heavy, tense air. "Tell him he was right, and thank you." He started for the door, then swung back around. "And tell him he's not to risk his own life or anyone else's coming after me." He nodded once, taking in both of them, and then disappeared into the dark corridor.

Aeshan struck out blindly, letting some of his fury escape with the pain that exploded as his knuckles contacted the bare wall. His headache surged, and dizziness engulfed him. It was well that he was already near the wall when the floor started spinning beneath him—he groped for the solid stone and leaned heavily, fighting the urge to swear in what had been a chapel. A hand gripped his shoulder.

"Sit."

He shook his head. "I'm fine, I—"

"*Sit*. You're not—"

"I don't *want* to sit!" he snarled, tearing away from Trevenorre's grasp and immediately stumbling into the rotting doorframe. Trevenorre's hand returned, and this time he managed not to push it away, not to yell at a king. "I apologize, your Majesty." He rested his forehead in the crook of his arm and breathed in deeply. "I had no intention of—"

"*Niha. Bae soin, bae quan.*" The quiet Elvesh words startled him, and calmed him enough to allow the dizziness to recede. Trevenorre's firm grip remained until he pushed away from the wall and stood straight under his own power. "You have been through a terrible ordeal, and you're in desperate need of food and water. It is unnecessary to stand on ceremony at this time."

Aeshan nodded his thanks, hating the weakness, the tremor in his hands and the hitch in his breath. "He's my sister's husband." He looked to Trevenorre, and caught the shadowed blue eyes with his own. "How can I just watch him walk away to his death? How am I to face my sister after that?"

"He's my son's friend, as well." Aeshan nodded, and pushed away the tension in his gut. He was in no mood to hear about just causes and necessary sacrifices. Trevenorre folded his arms across his chest and paced away. "Kethaloren . . . he's good with people, he's always been the one that every man, woman, and child in Rethalla felt they could approach in the streets and speak to as they would have one of their own. Ransanin was correct, though—Koren can and will treat with anyone, anywhere, but he guards his friendship very closely." He shook his head. "Less than a handful of people outside of our family have ever, over all of our years, been allowed casual use of Koren's family name."

Aeshan crossed his own arms, waiting, and when Trevenorre turned back, the blue eyes glittered with a hard, fierce light.

"Jase was correct. The three of us had no chance of rescuing the Lady and escaping alive."

He nodded, swallowing back the nausea. Would he ever be able to forgive himself? "Can you get us out without being seen? I know that—"

"The *three* of us had no chance." Trevenorre held up a staying hand. "Two of us, on the other hand, have much better odds. My son has no reason to be expecting me at all, and I doubt they will have brought the matter of a missing prisoner directly to him." A muscle jumped in his jaw. "He no longer seems the forgiving type."

Aeshan stared. "How could we—"

"We need to rest and regroup. You need a meal, perhaps two, and I need information."

"Is there time for that? We don't know—"

"There must be time." The king shook his head. "If we are to do this, we cannot rush it. Ransanin will not kill him right away. He wants information and I do not think Jase the type to quickly give it." Aeshan's stomach rolled again. Trevenorre nodded, as though he understood Aeshan's thoughts. "It will not be pleasant for him, but we must give ourselves a fighting chance. Moving too soon would be fatal for us all."

Aeshan surveyed Trevenorre, unable to quite believe what he was hearing. "What of Jase's request that we leave? You are important to those working to overthrow your son. What of—"

"It is a king's prerogative to decide his own priorities." Trevenorre offered a tight-lipped smile. "All that Jase said was correct, and the wiser course may indeed be to flee." He surveyed the ruined chapel again, and his eyes darkened. "But I will not be a man who leaves friends and women to suffer in the hands of a terror that I did not prevent." He saw Aeshan's glance, and smiled again, bitterly. "If we truly had no hope, I would leave. I'm not suicidal, and this isn't about vengeance." He crossed the stone tiles to stand directly before Aeshan. "No, with planning I believe this can be done. What say you?"

Disbelief and exhaustion and sheer adrenaline coursed through him. It was, perhaps, the stupidest thing he had ever contemplated, including the idiocy that had brought him here in the first place. But he was no longer in chains—he was free to make his own choices, free to risk his life for his family and for Rethalla's true king. He could feel the calm spreading through him, regardless of their dire circumstances.

"You truly believe that we have a chance?"

Trevenorre snorted. "Aye, I've said as much." He held out one hand—a Rethallan handshake, an offer of support and comradeship. "So, what say *you*?"

It was dangerous and ridiculous, but his heart was lighter than it had been in years, since before his capture and all that had followed. He didn't know if they could do this, if they truly had any chance at success, but Trevenorre believed they did and he wanted nothing more than to try. He threw caution to the winds, and grasped Tevlar Trevenorre's hand. "Very well. I'm in."

First-Flight Plight

Becca Lynn Rudder

The sun rose high, smiling over the land of Eranea. Many kinds of colorful flowers, such as fiddleneck, Ithuriel's spear, woodland star, and countless others, danced across the valley, and sparkling brooks ran hither and thither through it. The peaks of the Gwindes Mountains gleamed in the noon-day sunshine.

All of it seemed magical . . . which is not surprising, considering who the inhabitants of this land are. For this is a land of fairies, the very pixies that people love to dream about. I should know—I'm one of them. My name is Clirena.

It was a very momentous day in Eranea. Princess Argessa was about to fly for the first time, as this was her fifth birthday and her wings were finally big enough. Every fairy in the entire valley was preparing for the big celebration that would follow the Flight. All were anxious to witness such an event, though perhaps not everyone had the same reasons for their eagerness . . . .

I fluttered around, with furrowed brow. *Where could Eilia be?* I wondered. She wasn't at home. Could my little sister have gone to the King's Sequoia without me?

I was puzzling over this, when all of a sudden I was grabbed by the arm and spun around. "Whoa . . !" I exclaimed.

"Hi there, Clirena!" Eilia said as she finally stopped spinning me.

"What are me doing to you?! Wait . . . what?" I shook my head a couple times, trying to drive away dizziness.

Eilia giggled. "Nothing, but I think you said that wrong," she said with a grin.

"Oh, really?" I replied, a bit of sarcasm in my tone.

"M'hm!"

I sighed. "Never mind, Eilia. Where've you been? I've been searching every flower, tree, and berry bush for you!" I pointed at my little sister accusingly.

"I was at Kileri's Clarkia. You know that I promised to help her and Miss Laryn with decorations for today."

I blinked. "Kileri and . . . oh, right! Sorry, Eilia. I forgot about that."

"I noticed." Eilia smiled. "Come on, come on! We just *can't* be late!" With that, she grabbed my arm again and dragged me off to the Sequoia.

We got there not a moment too soon: the Princess was about to make her appearance! The King and Queen had just started their "proud of our little girl" speech when Eilia pulled me down into a seat next to her.

"Pixies and fae (that's "ladies and gentlemen," when humans say it), we thank you all for coming to this momentous event," King Carlor began. His wife, Queen Niriel, smiled brightly at the crowd gathered there for the occasion as he continued. "Today is truly a grand day in Eranea; young Argessa is about to perform First-Flight." Cheers rang out from just about every direction at that point.

When everyone had finally quieted down, Queen Niriel began to speak. "Our little daughter really is growing up swiftly. It seems like just yesterday, she wasn't even able to walk yet . . . " She smiled warmly at the memory for a moment, then swept her gaze across the crowd. "But now, she is getting ready to fly!"

"Yes, she will be out soon," King Carlor said. "But first, we must follow tradition. The Queen shall now sing of the first First-Flight."

This she did, but as it was of course in the language of Old Faer from ages gone by, which every fairy understands, though he or she cannot really find the words in newer languages to express what it means . . . I will not try to tell you what it said. All I can say is that when Queen Niriel sang it in her clear, sweet voice, everyone else fell utterly silent in awe.

When she finished, the King spoke once more. "Our little girl is almost ready, but before she takes flight, I would like her nurse to say a few words."

Well, let's just say that said nurse was rather shocked. I know this because that nurse was . . . well, me.

Like my mother and grandmother before me, I was one of the nurses of the Royal Nursery in the Sequoia. That said, I really was *not* expecting to be called upon to speak. I kind of stared for a moment and pointed at myself questioningly. The King and Queen just smiled and beckoned for me to come up to the balcony upon which they stood. I gulped, then complied—with a slight shove-out-of-the-seat from a grinning Eilia to help me do so.

I reached the balcony, trembling slightly as I bowed before the King and Queen. Queen Niriel put a gentle hand on my shoulder, whispered, "You can do it," in my ear, and then motioned for me to look out at the crowd and speak.

I looked out, but for a minute words escaped me—a minute which seemed like hours to me, but no one said anything about it, so it must not have been very long. Then I started, more because I had to do so than on having a clue about what to say.

"When Princess Argessa was born . . . " I began. Was that original? No. Was it expected? Well, from Eilia's horrible attempts at trying to hide a grin, probably. "When she was born," I said again, dragging my attention away from my little sister, "a crowd like this was also gathered for the event." I stopped. What did that matter? I wasn't trying to speak *then*. Think, Clirena, think!

"Be . . . because, it was also quite a momentous occasion," I continued attempting to save it. From the Queen's knowing, though encouraging, smile, I knew I wasn't doing a tremendous job as yet. "And, er . . . " A fellow nurse motioned for me to keep going, and I knew that meant "a couple minutes, dearie," as it came from the Head Nurse of the Nursery, Markette. A good, supportive mentor, but . . . that "couple minutes" didn't help.

I started to sweat a little. I'd never been a great public speaker, and everyone was watching me, boring into me with their eyes—or so it felt. Queen Niriel rested her hand on my shoulder and cleared her throat. "Well, I see that Argessa is ready," she said, gesturing to a lavender-pink flag that was the signal for "ready when you are." "Let's see our little girl fly, shall we?"

As the crowd cheered, she leaned over and whispered in my ear. "I asked Carlor not to make you give a speech, but he wouldn't listen. I am truly sorry that you had to go through that."

With an effort, I smiled. "It's all right," I whispered back. "At least it's over now. I may have just made a fool of myself, but that doesn't matter. This is the Princess' day; who cares what I did or didn't do for my speech?"

Queen Niriel laughed softly. "All right. Thank you for not being upset." She straightened up. "Now, if you are planning on watching my daughter's First-Flight, you had best get back to your seat." She smiled, then turned away to join the King in encouraging their daughter to fly.

I came back to my seat and sagged down into it. I couldn't believe that I'd just done that! Still can't, either, to be honest. Eilia looked over at me. "You all right?" she asked with concern in her eyes.

I smiled faintly. "Sure. Thanks for asking." Before she could say another word, I pointed at the balcony. "There she is!" I whispered as Princess Argessa walked out with her parents. For the moment, that kept Eilia's attention off me—and my attention off me, too.

Princess Argessa was a beautiful little girl. She had a pretty peach gown on and little white slippers. Her rose-gold circlet glimmered and gleamed in the afternoon sunlight, as well as her small, sparkling, silver-pink wings. She seemed rather nervous—understandable, considering she was very young, and this was the first time she'd be flying.

Now, don't mistake me, she had used her wings before. For a couple years now, we nurses had been having her try to hover a little to see how wing growth was coming along. Last time, she had nearly taken off around the room when she'd tried. So, of course, we knew she was ready, and that was why we were all at the Sequoia in the first place.

Queen Niriel gave her daughter a gentle nudge, and Argessa stepped forward to the edge of the balcony. I espied two or three Royal Guardians take positions around where she'd be flying, just in case it turned out that she *wasn't* quite ready, and they'd need to catch her.

Now, one of Princess Argessa's feet went over the edge. Everyone went utterly silent with eager anticipation. She pushed off the balcony with the other foot—Eilia grabbed on to my hand as if for dear life—and she was off.

Starting out, she fell a little ways, working her wings furiously. Then, she calmed herself and started to flutter her wings carefully. Now she was hovering. I watched silently, biting my lip. *Come on, go forward,* I thought at her anxiously.

She smiled, then kicked backward with her legs, fluttering her wings a little faster. She was actually flying. She was a little tilted to start with, and she had to figure out how to use her arms to help with balance . . . but she was flying!

Everyone cheered. Argessa had done it! She had performed her First-Flight! Pretty soon, she was flying around the trunks of trees and in and out of branches as if she'd been doing so her whole life. You could compare it to a bird, I suppose: never flew before, and then it did and it almost couldn't have done any better—after a bit of staggering and such, of course. That's how this was. Argessa was flying almost perfectly now!

And that's when the worst thing that could have possibly happened . . . *did*.

Suddenly, a rush like a whirlwind swept through the wood, bending several nearby trees, and breaking off branches—even one or two off the Sequoia. A heavy silence fell on us all, and we looked around anxiously for the cause of the wind. We didn't have to wait long.

We could see something darkling in the distance. It came upon us fast. When it stopped—right beside a very frightened young Princess—everyone gasped. It couldn't be . . . no, it just . . . it *couldn't* . . . but it was. A foe we thought had vanished forever had returned.

It was Dwimera, the most villainous fairy that I, at least, could recall. In a blue-black, sleeveless gown, her short black hair still whipping in a slight after-effect gale that remained for some time after the whirlwind had passed, she looked upon all of us with her nearly black eyes. After a moment, she spoke.

"So this is the young Princess I've heard so much about, hmm?" she said, looking a trembling Argessa up and down. Her voice was as darkling as her appearance.

Before she could get another word out, King Carlor flew toward them. "What are you doing back here? You said you would never return again."

"Oh, did I? Tsk, tsk, must have forgotten. Not that it matters. Did you *really* believe that, anyway? I have made such oaths before. All broken."

"I had hoped you had finally come to your senses. So much for that wish." King Carlor narrowed his eyes slightly. "What do you want with my daughter?"

Queen Niriel came up beside him. "That is a question I would very much like answered as well," she agreed in a surprisingly calm tone.

"Isn't it obvious?" Dwimera countered, gazing evenly at Niriel. "I came to complete a mission I've had for years. Didn't work with you, on the day of your wedding to Carlor here. Or several years before, with your mother when she had you, Queen Niriel." She grabbed Argessa rather roughly by the arm. "I thought perhaps a five-year-old would be easier." Her wings started to speed up again as she prepared to depart.

"No!" the King and Queen exclaimed. The Royal Guardians had silently surrounded Dwimera by now and were closing in.

Dwimera just laughed. "This old trick again? After a while, these things just don't work anymore." She flew straight up—still clutching Argessa—and got up to speed before the Guardians were even close. Another gust of wind—quite evidently produced by the tremendous rate at which her wings were fluttering—rushed through the wood, causing smaller trees to bend nearly double, some even to break. This time the whirlwind also knocked everyone to the ground!

I stood up as soon as I could, rubbing my shoulder and watching as the villain carried the young Princess away. I wondered where Argessa was being taken. What would Dwimera do to her?

What *could I* do?

* * * *

Young Argessa has been missing for several months now. Nobody's been able to figure out where Dwimera could have taken the little Princess. Queen Niriel is pretty much broken down, refusing to eat, drink, or even get out of bed. King Carlor is keeping his composure much better, but he's grown hard and stern as concern for his little daughter, and now his wife as well, consumes him more and more.

The Guardians say that they've looked everywhere; they've even posted a list of places they searched on a young sugar pine sapling near the Sequoia. I looked it over, and something about it confuses me: it lists everywhere that Dwimera's ever had a stronghold except for the old White Fir in the Black Forest where Dwimera started her villainy. I asked them about it, but they just gave me rather reticent looks.

"Everybody knows that her stronghold in that old tree was demolished years ago. There's nothing that could be there now," they told me.

"Shouldn't you check anyway?" I countered.

"Of course not! There is *nothing* there," they answered flatly. "Go on back to your work; there's nothing here for you to do."

I don't get that at all. Why won't they even consider looking? What's going on? Perhaps I should go talk to Markette about it. She's usually able to give obvious reasons to sometimes oblivious fairies . . . like me.

* * * *

My talk with Markette was rather interesting. She pointed out several things that I hadn't really thought about. Here's how it went :

I fluttered to the Royal Nursery, where I was sure I

would find Markette, as she of course is the Head Nurse there. It didn't take any searching to find her when I got there: she was hovering out in front of the Nursery, rubbing her chin with her hand. I knew that meant she was contemplating, and I was almost reluctant to interrupt her thoughts. Something good usually comes out of her contemplatings.

After a moment, however, I did interrupt. "Hello, Markette. I need to ask you something."

She jerked slightly. "Oh, goodness, dearie! Ye startled me." She smiled a little, rather sadly, it seemed to me. "But, that's all right, I suppose. I was only tryin' to think of what might be done about the darlin' little Princess. Silly ol' me, thinkin' I might be able to do somethin'!" she chortled.

"But Markette, you just might be able to! That's what I was going to ask you about!"

She pointed to herself. "Me? Oh, no, dearie, I don't see as how I could help."

I smiled. "We won't know unless we try, now will we?" Then I sobered again. "Markette, do you have any idea why the Guardians refuse to search the Black Forest for Princess Argessa?"

Markette paled slightly. "The Black Forest, eh?" she murmured. "Haven't heard that name in years, meself. Not for anything other than triumphant stories of its overthrow, leastwise." She looked me straight in the eye. "Now, Clirena, what made ye think of that, hrm?"

I shrugged. "I don't know for sure. I guess it's just because that was the one name *not* on the list of where they searched, and Dwimera *had* been there for a long time, even before anyone knew she'd turned to cruelty."

Markette nodded. "Aye, that's the truth. Used to go visit her at that White Fir she lived in, back when she was still one of the nicest fairies in Eranea." She smirked ruefully. "Hard to believe she was ever that, eh?"

I nodded in return. "Very. But, Markette, you haven't answered the question yet. Why won't the Guardians search there?"

She looked long and hard at nothing in particular, thinking on that. "Hrm, let's see now . . . the place does give near everyone the creeps, nowadays, even with the victory over it. The wildlife is right queer there, too. Didn't used to be. I wouldn't pass the thought of Dwimera helpin' that along. It could also be that no one thinks that she would be silly enough to go back to that ol' wreck of a hideout. Or . . . " She stopped, tilting her head.

"What is it? Or *what*, Markette?" I asked anxiously.

"Surely it's not that . . . but it could be," she murmured to herself.

"What, Markette, what?"

She looked at me again. "Ye've heard o' what happened when she first went cruel, haven't ye?"

I blushed a little. "Well . . . yes, but not for a long time, now."

Markette nodded. "Eh, it's not talked much about nowadays. I do have the sneakin' suspicion that it's part o' what's makin' the Queen so broke down now, though."

"What do you mean?" I asked, a little exasperatedly. Markette's a wonderful fairy, but she beats around the bush a bit too much at times.

"Well, dearie, it's like this. Many years ago, back when Queen Niriel was a wee baby, was the first time that any o' us knew anything about Dwimera's bein' evil. Don't give me that look! Dwimera's a mite older than me, aye, truth be told. I don't know how she hides it neither. Some sort of magic, for sure, but what kind I couldn't tell ye.

"Where was I . . . oh, o' course! Sorry, dearie, ol' minds'll wander on ye. Anyways, as I was sayin', it all started when Queen Niriel was itty bitty. In her mother Cilendra's weakened state—weakened, but *happy*, o' course!—Dwimera's true colors finally showed. She, with the help of a creature she called a—what was it now? Firanther, I think—kidnapped Cilendra and took her to the White Fir. At that time, no one thought of *her* possibly being in there, neither.

"Dwimera had cast some sort of spell over the King and Queen—King Carlor's parents, mind you. Even with all her usual regal air, Niriel wasn't born a Princess. Ah, there's a story and a half . . . but that's not what we're talkin' about, is it? Let's see . . . right, then. She put a spell on the King and Queen, Cilendra's family, the Royal Guardians, and any other fairies that she thought had brain enough to stop her.

"Truth be told, though, she should have put it on all o' us if she really wanted no one to find her. She's grown more clever since those days, but then she seemed to forget that me and several others that were her friends—a few that still are, poor, ignorant fairies—knew where she took abode and actually *did* have brain enough to figure it out on our own. This we did, but we couldn't get anyone else to believe us, save a few who, even under a spell, trusted us enough to still test our theories.

"We stormed that ol' White Fir, figured out how to break Dwimera's spell, and, well, the rest you know, the overthrow and banishin' of Dwimera."

Markette looked thoughtful again. "I suppose that could be it. I hadn't thought of that until we started talkin' about it just now."

I think my eyes must have lit up, or something, because Markette chuckled at me suddenly. "Don't get too excited, now, dearie. Might make ye lose yer head, and that won't help Argessa one bit."

I tilted my head. "What about Queen Niriel? Dwimera said that she'd tried with her, too. And what is she trying to do?"

Markette sighed. "Well, with Niriel, Dwimera didn't really have a chance to take her. Not the best to try *after* the weddin', better to do it durin' the ceremony, when everyone's staring at the soon-to-be partners in wedlock. Well, it's best to not do it *at all*, but you get my meanin', surely. Anyways, long story short, the Guardians captured Dwimera, locked her up, then poor King Carlor made the mistake of tryin' exile again instead of leavin' her in there.

"As for what she's doing . . . I don't rightly know, Clirena. I've thought of several things it could be, but none of them sound right, in my mind, anyways. Now," she looked at me evenly, "what are ye plannin' on doin', now that ye know 'bout all o' this, hrm?"

I pursed my lips. I really wasn't sure. "I-I ought to tell the King and Queen, shouldn't I?"

Markette gave me a knowing look. "Ye can try, dearie. Ye can *try*."

* * * *

This I did, but they *won't listen* to me. Most won't, anyway. Eilia, Kileri, Laryn—Markette, of course—and a few others are listening, but not many. Even the King and Queen themselves think that I've just gone half-crazy and won't even think of sending an expedition into the Black Forest to look for *their own child.*

Well, maybe I have gone mad. I don't care! I can't stand the thought of poor little Argessa in the clutches of that evil villain. I . . . I can't believe I'm saying this, but . . . I have to go to the Black Forest and look for her. I just have to, even if I must face Dwimera alone! I'm not going to let anything happen to my sweet little Princess.

I hope you'll wish me luck with this, friend.

I'm pretty sure I'm going to need it.

(The conclusion of this story, "A Pixie Rescue", will be included in *The Rudderhaven Science Fiction and Fantasy Anthology III.* I hope you enjoyed reading this story and will enjoy reading the next one, too!)

Out of the Tharonwood

S. L. Rudder

Alynniel was trying not to pace the room. After all, an Elf just did not behave in that impatient manner. She tried to lose herself in the magnificent view of Iniriand, deep in the heart of the Tharonwood, that spread out before her. Most times, especially at this time of the evening during the gloaming shadows of twilight, that view could take her breath away, but not this evening. Tonight, her brain just refused to slow down and drink in the beauty of the 'Wood. She turned back from the bay window that opened out onto the balcony of the sleeping quarters that she shared with her younger sister, Enyri.

Her sister! There she lay, draped across a lounge, so calm and serene. Lost in the wonders of the latest text that her mentor had given her. Enyri was studying to become a wizard's apprentice, and hours of endless delving into ancient scrolls and manuscripts seemed to fill her with nothing but contentment and joy.

Alynniel tossed her long, golden locks back over her shoulder with what could be considered nothing less than a purely impatient gesture.

It's so easy for her, she thought to herself. *She knows just exactly what path she is to follow in her life. Nothing is unsettled for her.*

Luckily for Enyri, Alynniel missed the amused look that crossed her sister's face as the blond Elfess turned back toward the window with a small huff. It would not have been in Enyri's best interest to have to explain that look to her sister with the mood she was in this evening. Best to let Alynniel work through this on her own, or at least wait until she was asked for her opinion.

Alynniel and Enyri were both young, by Elven standards, but most Elves had discovered their direction by this age. The fact that she was still searching might not have been so difficult for Alynniel if Enyri had not been chosen as a candidate for wizard's apprentice at such a young age. There were very few candidates chosen at all, and never had an Elf been selected before they had reached their third century up until now. Alynniel was very proud of her sister, and wished her well in her endeavors, but it all simply added to her own discontent.

No matter how hard she searched, it seemed as though Alynniel was destined never to find her place. As with all Elves, she was learned in lore and rudimentary healing, but sagely pursuits left her cold and looking for something more.

This Summer past, her parents had gifted her with a magnificent bow, *Wythring*. The bowyer of Telorin's court had labored for countless hours to fashion a bow that was as near perfection in both form and function as Elvenly possible. It truly was a thing of beauty, inlaid with gold, and shaped in a graceful curve. More and more she had taken to roaming the Tharonwood with *Wythring* and a quiver full of arrows. Hunting, yes, but more often simply trying to improve her shots until her skill surpassed that of the hunters in her father's court. Joining the ranks of the hunters held little or no interest for her, as much as she enjoyed the challenge of being deep in the heart of the 'Wood alone in pursuit of game.

Months at a time Alynniel would spend in solitude, building on her skill as a Ranger, taking to heart the lessons learned in the past and searching to find ways to improve on her own. Never satisfied with "good enough," always working to be better than she was the time before. She could identify and track any creature that she had ever come across in the 'Wood, even with the slightest spoor to follow.

Martial training with sword and shield was the only pursuit that brought her more joy than her sojourns in the 'Wood. When not out roaming, Alynniel would spend hours training at arms, taking all comers. Her skill had increased to the point where only Telorin and the greatest champions in the realm could hope to stand against her. In most cases it was only their greater strength that allowed them to overcome her, but at times her agility and stamina gave her the upper hand even with them.

While proud of her skill, Alynniel's parents often grew quiet and thoughtful as they watched her practice, a look of serene determination on her face. It was clear to them that their beautiful, golden-haired daughter was discontented with her life as it now was, and the skill she had gained with a sword caused them some trepidation when contemplating her future.

Alynniel's wandering thoughts returned to the present, and in order to keep herself from giving in to the temptation of pacing in an unelvish fashion, Alynniel retrieved *Wythring* from its corner near the balcony doors and prepared to return to the 'Wood to calm herself. As her hand grasped the latch of the outside door, there was a quiet knock at the chamber's entrance.

At the sound, Alynniel's hand dropped to her side, and she looked back across the room. From her place on the lounge, Enyri looked up, with a raised brow. She again attempted to hide a knowing smile, as the fist Alynniel had made slowly relaxed, and she walked across the room to answer the portal.

"My lady," the Elf addressed her. "Your parents request your presence in the main hall."

As Enyri prepared to rise, he motioned for her to remain where she was.

"Lord Telorin and Lady Celebriel request only Lady Alynniel to attend them at this time."

The younger Elfess' brow raised a bit higher as she resumed her place and looked toward her sister.

"What do you suppose this is about?" Alynniel asked her sister.

"I could not venture a guess," she replied. "It appears the best way to know is simply to let them explain it to you when you join them."

Thinking that younger sisters were little help, even if they were studying to be a wizard's apprentice, Alynniel returned her bow to its resting place and followed the courtier back to the main hall. Her mind raced with thought as to what this summons could mean.

Her guide opened the tall, inlaid double doors and motioned the young Elfess to proceed, as he bowed, turned, and departed.

Now that it was too late to change her attire, Alynniel glanced down and realized what she was wearing. She was dressed for the hunt, not to answer a summons from the Lord of Iniriand, even if he was her father. Her soft buckskin hunting tunic was tanned a rich, dark, golden brown, and trimmed with beautiful white fur. It was clean and tidy, as were her matching leggings, but hardly the formal attire that would be deemed proper for an audience with the Lord of Iniriand. She straightened her clothing as best she could, touched her hair where it waved around her face, then gave a small shake of her head and continued on to where her parents awaited her. This was far from the first time she had entered the great hall dressed in this manner.

Lady Celebriel was a vision, as always, in her soft flowing gown the color of moonlight, and Lord Telorin was quite handsome in his deep, forest green robe. Neither Lord nor Lady paid the least attention to how their daughter was attired. This was more a family meeting than a formal occasion, and they had assumed, that with the speed with which she had answered their summons, Alynniel would be dressed in just this manner. Both turned to greet her with love in their eyes, eyes that also gave hint to the seriousness of the situation.

The older Elves rose from their seats and left the raised dais at the head of the room. Lord Telorin guided his wife with a gentle hand on her back, and motioned his daughter to join them as they moved toward the richly padded benches near the roaring fireplace to one side of the hall.

"Alynniel, my dear," he greeted her as her mother gave her a tender embrace. "Come. Sit. Your mother and I have something of great import to speak of with you."

"Is there something amiss?" she asked as she took an uneasy seat on the front edge of the nearest bench.

"No, my darling," her mother's gentle smile allowed her to take a deep breath and relax into a more comfortable position. "Your father and I have just been discussing what course your life might take in the future."

Some of Alynniel's ease departed again with this comment, and she gave a minuscule twitch, but she was able to stop short of rising from the bench and pacing around the deep carpeting under their feet as she longed to.

A quick glance at her father was all it took to see that he well knew the predicament she found herself in. His deep blue eyes, so much like her own, twinkled with suppressed laughter. Yes, he knew his daughter very well, as did her mother.

"Relax, my dear," he said. "We are not asking you to choose a path this evening."

Lady Celebriel laid a gentle hand on her daughter's arm in reassurance. "We have just been observing you these last few seasons, and understand that you are still somewhat adrift."

"That is an understatement, Mother, to say the least."

"Your mother and I have been discussing this, and we feel that you may be putting too much pressure on yourself—trying to force your course and not let it extend out before you as it should."

Lord Telorin rose from his seat and moved towards the roaring fire. He spent a few moments gazing into its heart. Alynniel sat patiently, her eyes on her father's back.

"Your father and I both feel as though you are meant to have an important part in the future of Aaleria." Celebriel inserted quietly as she too watched her husband. She gracefully raised her hands, palms upwards, in an almost helpless gesture. "We are simply at a loss to know what that part may be."

Telorin turned back toward them as his wife spoke these words.

"Exactly!" he agreed. "Try as we might, we can come up with no way to assist you on your search.

"With your sister, 'twas simple. Even though she enjoys her time in the 'Wood, once she learned that she had an opportunity to be a wizard's apprentice, she could not find enough lore to study. She has a large portion of your mother's healing gift as well, and is most content with the path she has started on."

Alynniel fingered the stitching on the hem of her tunic. "Aye, contented she is. I left her with her nose deep in the latest scroll she has uncovered from the depths of your library." A wistful smile passed over the young Elfess' face. "I envy her her peace."

"Peace!" her father spoke into her musing. "My dear Alynniel, is there not a pursuit that grants you peace of any kind?"

"Only when I am out in the 'Wood. Deep amongst the trees, where the sunlight barely filters down, can I find peace. But it is fleeting at best."

Alynniel rose from her bench and made her way to the arched doorway leading out into her mother's favorite garden. She gently turned the latch and swung the doors wide, exposing the twilight view of the paths and planting beds.

"Especially at this time of night, when deep in the Wood. I can pause, close my eyes, and feel calm and at peace." She turned back to face her parents, the gloaming light bringing a warm, shimmering glow to her golden tresses. "Then in less time than it takes to tell you of this, that moment is gone and I feel as if there is something, I know not what, that is waiting for me so that it can be accomplished.

"I have the same feeling when I practice at arms. I am filled with a feeling I cannot describe every time I finally best a new opponent. It is not truly peace, or joy. It is more like a feeling of accomplishment in a list of unending tasks. Aah! This one is done. Then, it is on to the next!

"I have the same feeling when working with *Wythring*. Each mark hit, each target conquered, so much for that. Where will the next challenge be? I keep searching and searching, but I only find the next step toward the journey, not the quest itself."

Celebriel rose and moved to her daughter, pulling her into a warm embrace, saying nothing at that moment. She gently stroked her hair, comforting her with her calm presence, letting her love flow over her troubled child.

Alynniel clung to her mother for quite some time, memories of her youth streaming through her mind as she let her mother ease her feeling of lostness. Memories of the strength she always gained, the peace she obtained merely from her mother's love and presence. Nothing was too frightful or overwhelming if her parents were near.

Finally, Celebriel released her, and held her at arms length. There were tears glistening in her eyes as she turned them towards her husband. After receiving a warm look and slight nod from him, she said, "My darling, all this searching on your own to no end is too much for you."

She raised her hand, cutting off the comment her daughter was eager to make. "I know, we have taught you to be independent and self-sufficient. Somehow it always seemed that you would need those qualities more than most. But there are times when you must take help when it is offered."

Telorin smiled at them both. "And take that help with no questions, whether or not it is desired, for more often than not you will find that it was just what you were in need of, without even knowing it."

Alynniel's gaze returned to the garden now bathed in moonlight. Her parents were both so wise. Never in the past had she disregarded her parents' advice. This time would not be the first. She slowly made her way back to her bench. Her demeanor telling them as clearly as words that she was ready and willing to listen to any help they could give her.

Lord Telorin clapped his hands and a pair of attendants entered the hall, each bearing a package in their hands. One bore a large bundle wrapped in deep purple cloth and tied with a silver cord. This he placed near the hearth, leaning up against a pillar. The second carried a vibrant blue velvet pillow with a golden satin napkin draped over it. Celebriel received this and placed it gently on a small stool sitting near the bench she was seated on. Both attendants left the hall, closing the door behind them in complete silence.

The silver cord and golden satin reflected the firelight, seeming to burn and glow themselves. The Elflord placed his hand on the top edge of the large bundle, running his hand gently back and forth as he gathered his thoughts. Then, reaching a decision, Telorin inclined his head ever so slightly toward his wife.

Lady Celebriel retrieved the blue pillow then turned to Alynniel, holding it on her lap. Alynniel's eyes widened in wonder as her mother lifted the golden covering. Resting atop the pillow was a narrow golden circlet, open at the back so as to fit above the brow and under the wearer's hair. Simple, without engraving or filagree of any kind, it was polished until it was as smooth and perfect as a mirror. In the center, where it would rest upon one's forehead, was a beautiful blue beryl, the size and shape of a robin's egg. It's color was the deepest blue that Alynniel had ever seen in such a stone. Not as dark as a sapphire, but a deep rich blue with just the slightest touch of green to it. The exact color of the lake deep in the heart of Tharonwood where it reflected both the sky and the trees that surrounded it. The quality of the stone was unparalleled and it glowed with an inner light all its own.

Celebriel lifted the circlet and placed it on her daughter's brow. The stone's glow intensified, then waned as the Lady removed her hands from it.

"The stone in this circlet has long been treasured by the Elves," Celebriel spoke in her soft, gentle voice. "It has been in your father's keeping now for many centuries. It is a 'blessed' stone, given into the keeping of the Elves since Aaleria first came into being. It is called '*Lureliare*,' the love-link stone. It forms a connection or link between its bearer and all those who share a pure and undying love with them.

"The increased glow it gave off as we were both touching it was caused by the deep love I have for you, my darling. The same would be true should you and your father, sister, or any other member of our family touch it at the same time. As long as you bear it, we will always know how you fare, if you are well or if you are in danger or injured, though it cannot tell us what might be wrong, nor can it tell us where you are."

Lord Telorin broke in at this point, "It gives more of a 'feeling' as to what is occurring to the bearer than actual facts. Those who love you will be able to feel what you are feeling, be it happiness or pain, but not know the cause."

Clebriel nodded. "The strength of the link is in proportion to the strength of the connection between you and the other person. Your father and I will always be able to feel it, unless some evil power were great enough to sever the link. Your sister may well find times when she cannot feel you, but she will be able to tell that you still bear the stone."

"Yes," Telorin continued, "as long as you bear the stone, we all shall know. Only you yourself will be able to remove the circlet now that it is attuned to you. Only your death would allow another to remove it, and at that point the stone will cease."

Alynniel's eyes grew with wonder, as she raised her hand and caressed the smooth surface of *Lureliare*. To be entrusted with such a gift was a humbling experience for the young Elfess, and she would not treat the privilege lightly. Never had she thought to possess a "blessed" stone. There were so few of them left in Aaleria and each one was "blessed" for a specific task.

Before Alynniel had time to ponder on what this might mean, her father moved to the larger bundle resting near the fire. He gently untied the cord and pulled it loose. As he did this, the purple cloth fell free, revealing a fine Elven sword and shield. Just the sight of them caused Alynniel's hands to ache to try them.

The shield was rounded at the top and came to a gentle, rounded point at the bottom. It curved in slightly on both sides just above where the bearer's arm would be. It was banded in gold and had a deep green background that made the cluster of golden Aspen leaves stand out in bold relief in the center. The sword had a long narrow blade and the hilt and guard were also over-laid with gold. The open filagree of the guard sported golden Aspen leaves as well, and there was a deep green beryl set in the pommel. The scabbard and belt were of beautifully wrought work. Alynniel could tell that Telorin's weaponsmasters had been hard at work once again.

Smiling at the look of longing on his daughter's face, Lord Telorin handed her the sword and shield.

"This shield is *Falorn*, and the sword, *Angil*."

He gave a small chuckle as her eyes grew even wider when she felt the balance of the weapon and the lightness of the shield.

"Father," she breathed, barely loud enough to be heard, "I have never seen their equal! I do not understand why you are giving me these lavish gifts, but I shall treasure them always."

A look of sadness entered her father's eyes as he took a seat near his wife and daughter.

"My dear Alynniel, I am grateful that these gifts bring you such joy, but love for you alone is not the reason they have been given. As your mother mentioned earlier, we have encouraged your independence since your birth. We have always known that you were meant for some special task."

Celebriel spoke up as he paused. "We do not know what that task may be, but the feeling of urgency to prepare you for it has been increasing steadily these last few seasons. That is why your father commissioned these gifts for you."

Lord Telorin nodded his head in agreement. "Yes, and now we have received a message from Indariel in Valamar. She requests you to journey to her. You are to leave within a fortnight and make your way to her. I know not the reason she has sent for you, only that you are called and therefore must go. Two more instructions did she send to you. 'Travel by the upper path, but pass not through the land of Avilar' and 'Take no mount as you depart.' I know not why she has put forth these stipulations, but you must follow them in your journey.

He smiled tenderly at his daughter. "Take care of any parting wishes you may have, and prepare to depart as soon as you are able."

"Always know that your father and I will be thinking of you, my Darling," Lady Celebriel's beautiful eyes were brimming with tears, "and that as long as you wear *Lureliare* we will know how you are faring."

Dawn of the following morn found Alynniel many miles into her journey, nearing the edge of the 'Wood and eager to be on her way. She found it strange to feel such a mix of anticipation and peace. Knowing that Indariel of Valamar could well be the guide to her life's path made her spirits lift and calmed her doubting heart.

Even with her anxious feelings, and the need for haste, Alynniel found the Ranger in her coming to the fore as she left her beloved 'Wood for the rolling hills and meadows of Wintly. Scattered across the plains were many small villages and hamlets. In the mornings, smoke rose from the chimneys of these as the Sun rose higher in the sky. The young Elfess found herself wishing she had the time to explore one of these small villages as she made her way quietly past them. She could hear the sounds of people starting about their days, the blacksmith's hammer ringing on his anvil, a merchant calling out good-mornings to all who passed by as he swept the porch and steps of his store, children calling to each other as they went about their adventures. Added to the sounds were the smells of bread baking, wood smoke from the fires, and the stables that had been mucked out before breakfast.

Alynniel had not had much contact with the race of Men and longed for a chance to meet and study them. Their cobblestone roads and log or stone houses were such a contrast to the Elven halls of her father. For many seasons now, she had longed to know what these people that were so similar to yet so different from her own were truly like. She shared this longing with her sister once, but the look she received in return was most unsettling. Enyri appeared to be about to say something, but then it was as if the thought had vanished as soon as it was formed. After that, Alynniel kept her thoughts on the subject of Men to herself.

Each small hamlet she passed by was surrounded by equally small farms. Crops were beginning to grow in their patchwork fields. Animals were going about their business in their pens and enclosures.

The Sun had passed its nooning one bright day as Alynniel was preparing to skirt yet another of these domiciles when she noted that its inhabitants were climbing into a two-wheeled cart drawn by a small, sleepy looking donkey. She paused in the shadow of a copse of willows on the edge of a nearby stream. The donkey slowly plodded away down the dirt road towards the nearest village, and Alynniel, her curiosity at its height, could not resist the temptation to explore!

As the cart and its occupants made their way from sight over the top of a small hill, Alynniel glided through the shadows of the hedges that grew near the road and then behind a wooden pen that housed a few bleating sheep until she reached the back corner of the stone stable. She listened intently for a few moments. Being satisfied that there was no Man present, she stepped around the corner and entered the small building. A brown and white spotted milch cow lay chewing her cud in contentment, the bell around her neck jingling softly, as her young calf frolicked around her stall. Chickens clucked and scratched around the door, and a pair of good sized hogs had their noses buried deep in a trough of slop.

Alynniel took just a few moments to thoroughly investigate every bag, barrel, and corner of the dim interior, pausing only once to smile down on the mother cat and kittens that she discovered in a back corner behind some wooden crates.

Checking her surroundings carefully, Alynniel moved across the yard. She looked longingly at the small cottage, then up the dirt road in the direction the cart had disappeared. Even knowing she should not do so, the Elfess made her way to the door of the dwelling.

Listening carefully for any sound, she gently edged it open. Total silence met her as she peered through the crack, and with one more quick glance down the road, she made her way inside, leaving the portal open to aid her hearing the family's return.

Alynniel stepped to the side of the doorway, leaving her pack and weapons near it in case she needed to leave quickly. Her eyes filled with wonder as they traveled around the one-room dwelling. The far wall contained a fireplace, coals of the banked fire giving off a soft glow. Near it, on the right-hand wall and under the home's only window, was a small table with a stool at each end and benches pulled up to the longer sides. Pegs beside the hearth and hooks on a frame near it held a wonder of cooking utensils the likes of which she had never seen. The larger pieces, evidently intended for preparing stews and such like, were made of a black, rough metal. The spoons and dippers were carved from wood, crude to her Elven eyes, but serviceable. On a small set of shelves she found bowls and cups that appeared to be shaped from hardened gourds. There was also a small stack of bags, boxes, barrels, and objects she longed to know the use for in the corner between the table and the hearth.

Alynniel wished to investigate as thoroughly here as she had in the stable, but the fear of the family's return caused her to move on to the other side of the cottage. Here she found a sturdy wooden bed. The coverings were coarser than the silks and linens she was accustomed to, but appeared to be very warm.

In the back corner, she could see a ladder leading up through an opening in the ceiling. She had come this far, and the Elfess did not even hesitate before ascending its rungs. Her eyes sparkled with delight as she discovered a small, low loft. One side contained baskets of root vegetables, sacks of coarse flour, and other foodstuffs. The other side, above the fireplace below, had a row of four small sleeping pallets, each with a small wooden box at its head. Alynniel raised the lid of the first box, and discovered the treasures of a small boy, pieces of colorful rock, a lumpy home-made ball, and many bits and pieces that she could not identify with her brief look. With a tender smile she closed the lid, and even though she longed to discover what each box held, made her way back down the ladder.

Alynniel's eyes swept the cottage to make sure that there was no hint of her presence and, picking up her belongings, she quietly exited and closed the door. She was surprised at how much time had passed while she was exploring the dwelling. The Sun was sinking slowly toward the distant rocky hills as she made her way further from the farm to a small stand of timber along the stream. As she faded from sight under the overhanging limbs, her ears picked up the squeaking of the cartwheels and children's laughter as the family made its way home from the village. A slightly sad smile crossed her face as she gave a small half-shrug and continued on with her journey. It would have been such a delight to watch them for even a short time, to see how this family interacted with each other.

As the days passed, Alynniel left the meadows of Wintly for the rugged steppes and scattered forests of the Collester Hills. While there had been no shortage of wildlife on the plains, here the Elfess saw a greater variety of tracks and animal dwellings. Her hunter's eye cataloged each as she passed by without even slowing her stride. This lively forest was far different from her more peaceful 'Wood, but many of the creatures were the same.

Darkness was falling one evening and she was preparing to make camp and a small evening meal. Making her way to a stream of cold, crystal clear water gurgling over a rocky bed, Alynniel came upon some unexpected sign. There on the rocky bank lay a small wooden bucket, and she could see where something large had fallen. There were displaced stones and rocks and blood spattered about on the sparse bushes growing nearby. After caching her pack, bow, and shield in the branches of a nearby tree, the Elfess, *Angil* at her side, carefully checked the area, both looking and listening for anything that seemed out of place. She then examined the site of the fall and discovered that there had been two different beings involved. Leading up to the place from the northeast, there was a faint trail which had been made by a Man. Off to the left of this path, she found where a very large creature had lain in wait and then lunged at its prey leaving deep gouges in the damp earth. The Man had fought back, for she could trace quite a battle through the underbrush.

Alynniel, her hand ready at her sword, expected to come upon a dead body right away as she followed the path of the fight through the underbrush. She was extremely surprised when she did, and it was not the Man. There lying dead, its carcass sliced to ribbons, was one of the biggest vargs that the Elfess had ever seen. The varg, a creature of Evil, looked much like a wolf, but was approximately twice the size and weight and more than ten times as vicious. This one had been dead now for at least a day. Its throat was nearly sliced through, and there was the broken blade of a dagger sticking out of its side just behind its left front leg. With a contemplative look, Alynniel continued to track the other combatant.

The trail was easy to follow, and with as much blood as the man had lost the Elfess held out little hope of finding him alive. She could see where he had dragged himself along, and also where he had fallen and lain still for long intervals before moving on once more. The Man had made it back to the pathway coming from the stream, and Alynniel came upon him lying there as if someone had dropped him on his face just feet from the door of a hunter's cabin. One arm, the hand still clutching the haft of the broken dagger, stretched out towards it.

Tentatively, she approached him and was relieved to find that the Man was still breathing. Knowing that there was little she could do for him there on the path, she made her way up to the cabin to see what she could find. She opened the cabin door, her curious eyes darting everywhere to take in as much as she could at first glance.

There were two narrow beds, a small table with two stools, and a small stone fireplace. One wall was covered with animal traps and there was a pile of freshly fletched arrows at one end of the table. Alynniel pulled back the covering of animal skins on one of the beds and went back outside. Staggered by the Man's weight, she finally managed to lift him enough to half-drag, half-carry him into the cabin. She hoisted him onto the bed, then lit the fire that was laid ready on the hearth to help warm up the room. On the table sat a small lamp; lighting this, she moved back to the occupied bed to examine the unconscious Man. His right leg was broken, most likely from the impact of the varg's opening attack. His left arm was deeply lacerated and bruised as if he had forced it back into the varg's jaws to hold them away from himself. Alynniel gently pried the broken dagger out of the Man's right hand. That arm was also covered with blood, but most of it belonged to the varg. She laid the broken haft on the table, pulled the coverings up over the Man's chest, and then left to retrieve *Wythring, Falorn,* and her pack from the tree where she had left them. As she went, she fetched the bucket and filled it with water so that she could cleanse his wounds.

Upon her return, Alynniel cast around outside the cabin to check what sign she could find. From the tracks she discovered, two Men shared the cabin, but there were no tracks less than a week old for the second Man. She would have to keep a watch out for his return.

After a quick check on her patient, the Elfess began heating water in one of the strange black pots similar to the ones she had seen at the farmstead. She then went into her pack to find the medicinal herbs she carried with her. Some of these she made into a poultice, others she placed to steep in a bowl of the water she had heated over the fire. When this was accomplished, her next course of action was to set the broken leg-bone. The Man gave a weak groan during this process, but did not regain consciousness. As she cleansed the wounds, she found that the lacerations on his left arm had started to infect, and she applied the poultice she had made before bandaging it.

When she had made him as comfortable as she could, Alynniel took the time to do some exploring both inside and outside of the cabin. In a lean-to on the backside of the dwelling she found bundles of furs and skins the hunters had collected. Nearby were frames holding a number that were still in the process of being tanned. She spent quite some time examining the various tools she found. While the Men's technique was different from her own, she found that the end result was quite passable.

Moving out into the trees surrounding the small clearing, Alynniel scouted for signs of either the second Man or any possible foes. Finding nothing to cause her alarm, she returned to check on the wounded hunter. The Man remained unconscious, so she administered the tea she had left steeping, made sure he was warmly covered, and continued her exploration inside.

The contrast between this dwelling and the cottage she had seen before were striking, but not surprising to one who had spent much time in Elven hunting cabins. The farm had been home to a family with many touches to add warmth and comfort. This was the abode of two working hunters. It was filled with the tools to help them do their job with little room for anything else. The same contrasts could be made between similar Elf dwellings. Home was where you could find comfort, though most of the Elf hunters Alynniel had ever worked with tended to bring as much comfort with them when out in the 'Wood as they could. These Men seemed to be content with just the bare necessities.

Alynniel checked on the hunter again, and began cleaning up around the bed. When she bent down to pick up a soiled rag that had dropped to the floor, she saw the corner of a small box with a cloth napkin peeking out of it. She pulled it out for a better look. Folding back the napkin, she found it contained small clusters of nuts that were held together with a honey mixture of some kind. Unable to resist, she broke off a tiny piece and tasted it. Her eyes closed as a small smile played across her face. These were wondrous! Evidently Man hunters liked their little comforts too.

For the next two days Alynniel cared for the hunter, treating him with herbs, and feeding him with a broth she made from some dried, smoked meat she found among the cabin's stores. She was greatly relieved when the inflamation and infection went down in his arm, and also when his breathing became less ragged. He did not fully regain consciousness but did seem to be getting stronger, and her hope was he would awaken soon.

As the wounded hunter lay there resting, she would spend time simply gazing at him. Never had she been so close to any of the race of Man, and here was one she could study to her heart's content. The hunter had dark hair, and was much heavier than an Elf would have been at the same height. During her examination, she had found that he had warm, brown eyes with just a touch of amber to them. She knew from talking to Elves that had been much in the Man world, that they often found Men's looks to be coarse in comparison to their own. Alynniel did not find them so. She thought his looks more rugged, but not unappealing. She hoped that he would awaken soon so that she would have a chance to speak with him and possibly gain answers to her many questions, but as that thought crossed her mind she knew it could not be. She must continue her journey to Valamar as soon as she was able to leave him on his own.

On the morning of the third day, the Elfess was in the timber near the cabin gathering some berries, when she heard someone rushing up the path from the stream calling, "Bernard, Bernard, are you here?" She quickly dashed back into the cabin to retrieve her belongings, then made her way out the door and into the trees on the side opposite the path. A large, dark-haired Man burst into the clearing. From his looks, Alynniel believed that he and the Man she had been caring for were brothers. A soft reply came from inside the cabin showing that the wounded hunter was awake, and the Elfess quickly continued on her journey. She could not help but wonder how the Men would explain her care of the wounded Bernard. She would have liked to stay and introduce herself to them, but she had already lost more than two days from her journey. Perhaps someday she would get the chance to actually speak with a Man. The questions she had long had about their world only became larger and more numerous the closer she came to it.

Alynniel broke out of the timber on a craggy cliff near the edge of the Hills. Before her lay the rolling prairie pastureland of Smead. From her vantage point, the Elfess could see a great herd of horses feeding below, several Men watching over them and others around a small camp near a stream bed. Even in Iniriand they prized the mounts of Smead for their beauty, speed, and stamina. She longed to sit and watch both the steeds and their keepers, but knew she must continue on. With an impatient shake of her golden head, she turned to find a way down from the heights and on into Smead itself. In the distance past the herders, she could just make out a village or town. It appeared to be much larger than any she had come across in Wintly, but she dare not take time for more exploring now.

As Alynniel descended from the heights and crossed over into the land of Smead, she became aware of a slight, nevertheless pressing, unsettled feeling. It was a feeling that she could not explain, even to herself. It was not danger or fear, nor was it excitement or anticipation. It was more like a change in the air around her in some way that had nothing to do with the wind currents or even possible odors. Something was simply different and beyond her power to comprehend at that moment. This feeling seemed to grow the farther she ventured into the kingdom.

As she made camp for the night on a hilltop overlooking a large keep nestled in the valley several miles below, the feeling grew ever so slightly stronger. Trying to ignore it, she settled down beneath a tall oak tree to try to get some rest before continuing her journey at dawn's first light.

As she closed her eyes, Alynniel thought she saw a slight blue glow on her crossed arms she was using to pillow her head. Her eyes shot wide open, but she could see nothing other than the gloomy shadows of the branches overhead. The eerie feeling that had pressed in on her from the time she had entered this land must be affecting her imagination.

After making certain that sword, shield, and bow were within easy reach, she closed her eyes once again and let her mind flow into Elven rest.

The next day, long before the sun had risen over the Collester Hills now far behind her, Alynniel continued her journey. The unexplained feeling seemed to lessen with every stride she took nearer the far border. The young Elfess was as confused by this as she had been by the sensation's growth when she had entered Smead.

Yet one more question to seek an answer for when I reach Valamar, she thought to herself as she made her way into the edge of the Graden Hills.

Alynniel took her nooning amid the rocks and boulders that surrounded the higher peaks she could see in the distance. She carefully let her eyes roam over both the land and the sky as she checked each of her weapons to make sure they were free from dust and ready to use. She even took the precaution of stringing her bow and drawing a pair of arrows from her quiver to carry ready in hand.

There was a dragon that lived in the Graden Hills, and while not one of the largest in all of Aaleria, it was nonetheless a threat to be prepared for. Many an Elven scout had relayed tales of the beast while reporting to her father's court. The Men who lived near the dragon's hunting grounds had even taken to setting traps, hoping to capture and destroy it. So far, to no avail.

Even though she had full faith in her skills both as a Ranger and a warrior, Alynniel had no wish to face even a lesser dragon on her own if she could avoid it. She knew that if she were able to slay the dragon, she would undoubtedly be severely wounded in the encounter, and her chances of living to tell her tale would be very slim.

Sunset was approaching as the Elfess carefully made her way deeper into the Hills. She thought she heard a thrashing coming from a copse of trees she could see in the distance. Curious, as only a young Elf female could be, she slowly made her way forward, pausing often to look and listen. If one of the Men's traps had actually managed to capture the dragon, she wanted to know it long before she reached it. Knowing a dragon's great cunning and strength, she highly doubted this was the case. That and the fact that she could not hear the dragon-like roars and growls that would most assuredly accompany such an inconvenience.

Hoping to gain a better view in the growing twilight, Alynniel scrambled up into a tall pine nearby. From that vantage point she could see that the tops of several huge pine trees farther up the hillside were bent down as if anchored to the earth beneath. Again the thrashing sounded, and the trees jumped and pitched as if dancing. This action was accompanied by a cry of distress. Alynniel's blue eyes widened as she realized the call sounded much like a horse. A horse in the treetops? That was impossible!

Moving as quickly as caution would allow, she made her way back to the ground and on toward the disturbance ahead. As she drew nearer, the thrashing lessened, but the cries increased.

"*Please, you must help me!*"

Alynniel stopped dead in her tracks, giving her head a slight shake of bewilderment. Her ears still heard the wicker of a horse, but she could hear the meaning in her mind!

"*Please don't stop! You must hurry before the others return,*" was neighed into her thoughts.

"Who or what are you?" She carefully made her way nearer. "And who are the others?"

The thrashing about had almost come to a complete stop by this point, and the "voice" was much calmer and somehow clearer in her mind.

"*The others are the Men who laid this trap that I have had the misfortune to become entangled in. As to who or what I am, that must wait until you have freed me from this snare.*"

Alynniel, with all the caution a Ranger Elf could muster, made her way quickly and silently toward the trap.

She paused in astonishment when she finally reached it. There, twenty feet above the ground was a huge net. From her vantage point there below and in the growing darkness, she could not see how it was holding its prey. What she could see was a silvery, grey tail and a pair of hooves that could only belong to a horse! A horse in the treetops!

"Maybe the horse was somehow used as bait for the trap," she thought to herself, "and there is another 'being' of some kind in there now also."

"Are you in there with the horse?" she asked as she completed her circuit around the area beneath the dangling net, trying to find some way to lower it.

"*No,*" came the neighed thought. "*I am the horse, in a way.*"

Alynniel was so intrigued by this point that she could barely stand it.

"In a way?" she questioned.

"*Well, yes,*" came the reply. "*Release me from this mess, and I promise you I will be more than willing to explain it all to you.*"

"Very well, but this may take some doing."

The young Elfess climbed up each of the four anchor pines and was not long in figuring out the Men's snare. It was simple, yet ingenious at the same time.

"Prepare yourself, I will attempt to lower you now."

A pleased sounding wicker was the only reply at this point, but she was afraid that it sounded much weaker than at first.

Alynniel was able to lower the net, then pulled out her dagger to release the captured victim.

"Hold tight, I am going to try to cut you loose as quickly as I can."

There was a soft affirmative nicker, then all struggling ceased.

Darkness had completely fallen by this time, and even Alynniel's Elven eyes were having trouble seeing in the gloom as she worked. She cut through the thick roping as carefully and quickly as she was able.

"One more strand, and I think you should be able to shake yourself free."

As the last strand parted, she stepped clear of the net and peered into the gloom, trying to see what this "in a way" horse looked like.

The captive dislodged the netting as it surged to its feet with a loud neigh and a flutter of wings.

Wings?!

"*I'm free!*" came to Alynniel's mind as she stood there speechlessly watching the creature come towards her. It was a beautiful silvery white all over. Or was it silvery grey? It spread out a pair of powerful-looking wings of the same coloring as if testing them for injury. Moving toward her, it passed through the shafts of moonlight glimmering between the tall pines. This caused the creature to shimmer with an inner glow, much like the young Elfess herself. Then, as it made its way into the deeper shadows, it seemed to blend into them, becoming hard to distinguish from them.

It is something of note for any Elf to be caught flat-footed and speechless, but Alynniel would have sworn that during all of her wanderings she had seen everything there was to see in all of Aaleria, and that nothing could take her by surprise. But, there standing before her was a creature straight from ancient myths and legends told of a time when Aaleria was young.

"Why, you, you are a . . . a . . ."

"*Mahur,*" the being finished her statement for her as it drew close enough to snuffle at her arm, its magnificent wings folded close to its side.

Without the wings, the Mahur would have been the most beautiful stallion that Alynniel had ever seen. Taller at the withers than the Elfess herself, he was very powerfully built with a deep chest, trim legs, clean lines, small sound feet, and a lovely head with a slightly concave profile. His eyes were amazing! They were a deep sapphire blue, and held an intelligence far above that which any animal should have been capable of.

Almost of its own volition, Alynniel's hand reached up to stroke the velvety muzzle. She spoke, her voice hushed with awe, "Where did you come from? What are you doing here?"

The Mahur rubbed his muzzle against the Elfess' cheek, and gently blew a warm breath on her neck. A giggle of pure joy escaped Alynniel before she could pull her warrior training to the fore.

"*Where I have come from, that I can not tell you,*" was nickered into her thoughts. "*As to what I am doing here, I have been searching for my Companion. And now I have found her.*"

Alynniel stepped back in surprise. "Companion? Found her? Whatever do you mean?"

The sapphire eyes seemed to glow more intensely as the Mahur gazed at the Elfess.

"*I was sent forth on a quest to find my Companion. You are my Companion.*"

"I am your companion?" Alynniel began to pace quickly back and forth in the dimming twilight. "What do you mean, I am your companion?"

"*If you will please hold still, I will attempt to explain.*"

Alynniel stopped short. Pacing again! At least Enyri was not here to see.

"*Much better. Each Mahur who is sent forth into your world must find their Companion in order to remain here. You can hear my thought talk, this means that you are my Companion. No other would be able to understand me.*"

So many questions began circling around in the young Elfess' mind that she could not voice even one. She slowly sank down onto the thick covering of pine needles, shaking her head as she stared at the living myth before her.

"*Companion, are you harmed? Are you in need of assistance?*"

This inquiry seemed to bring Alynniel back to the present.

"No, I am quite well."

"*I am pleased, Companion. It would be most distressing if I were to lose you where I have just now found you.*"

Alynniel's sense of humor bubbled forth at this point. Having a mythical creature calling one "Companion" struck her as incredibly funny, and she laughed up into the serious face above her. "My name is Alynniel. I would be most pleased if you would address me so. Being called 'Companion' seems most strange."

"*Very well, then that is what I shall call you.*" The Mahur tipped his head slightly to one side; "*Alynniel. Yes, that is just what I shall call you!*" The creature gave a pleased-sounding snort and raised up into the air with a thrust of his wings.

"*Alynniel is the name of my Companion!*" he whinnied as he flew in a tight circle then settled back to the ground.

"*A most beautiful name for a most beautiful Elf!*" came happily into Alynniel's mind.

"Why thank you," she said with a slight bow of her head. "Now, what is your name? What am I to call you?"

The Mahur folded his wings, and his head drooped ever so slightly.

"*There is no way for me to make you understand what I am called. It cannot be said in 'thought talk' it can only be spoken with my voice. Perhaps you can tell me what you would like to call me.*"

Alynniel rose gracefully from her seat on the ground. Without even attempting not to do so, she began to pace back and forth there under the trees, her speed increasing with each turn. How on Aaleria did one go about naming a creature of legend and myth?

Her movements seemed to fascinate the Mahur, and he lay himself down, fluffing his wings around him, eyes following the Elfess' progress back and forth in the shadow of the pines. The longer Alynniel paced, the more intently the Mahur watched, and the more intently the Mahur watched, the longer Alynniel paced.

Finally, coming to a sudden stop, the Elfess turned to study the creature before her. The moonlight filtering down between the branches playing across his coat and wings caused the Mahur to glow and glimmer like twilight.

"That is it!"

The Mahur jerked his head back, startled by the outburst.

"*That is what?*"

"That is what I shall call you! Twilight! You shimmer and glow just like a beautiful twilight in the Tharonwood. That would be the perfect name for you."

The Elfess stepped forward and once again gently stroked the soft, velvet muzzle.

"Twilight in the Tharonwood," she murmured. "The most beautiful of all times of the day. The time that has always seemed so fleeting and that I never want to pass."

"*Twilight?*" the Mahur seemed to test the name. "*I would be honoured to bear this name knowing it means so much to you. Twilight is now what I shall be called!*" And with that, Twilight extended his wing and drew Alynniel into an embrace. The Elfess threw her arms around the powerful, arched neck beside her, and returned the embrace.

"*I have found both my Companion and my name. Now I can continue my quest.*"

Alynniel stepped back, the easier to see Twilight's face. "You still have a quest?"

"*Yes. My quest is to stay with you always and assist you on yours. We are now 'Companions.' That is a bond that only death can break.*"

Alynniel shook her head ruefully, turned her back, and took a few steps into the surrounding gloom.

"If only I knew what my quest might be!"

Twilight surged to his feet and came up behind the Elfess, silently resting his head on Alynniel's shoulder. Alynniel reached back and placed her hand against the Mahur's cheek, hugging his face against her own.

"*Perhaps we can discover that together,*" he gently wickered into her mind.

For the first time in more seasons than she could remember, a feeling of peace wash over her as she and Twilight made their way deeper into the forest. They moved away from the trap, and anyone who might come to check it, to a place where they could rest. Dawn was not many hours away, and then they could continue on to Valamar in Pekka together, two Companions.

Alynniel awoke with a giggle as Twilight once again blew softly on her neck. The Mahur had decided that was a lovely sound, and took every advantage he could to hear it. They found a nearby stream, and Twilight grazed on the thick grass growing on its banks as Alynniel prepared her own small breakfast. She was eager to reach the end of her journey now that it was so close.

In between bites, the Companions discussed the best route to take to Valamar. Alynniel had been there many times, but never had she approached from the Graden Hills. The normal path of the Elves led through Avilar, but she had not followed it because of Indariel's instructions.

"It should at most be only two more days," Alynniel said thoughtfully. "I am sure that you will have no trouble keeping pace with me." She turned to look more closely at the Mahur. "Although, your size will mean that we will not be able to take some of the pathways I would take if I were on my own. Your wings will make ducking through close-lying bushes more difficult."

"*Well then, why do I not just fly us there?*"

The Elfess paused with a bite halfway to her mouth, slowly dropped her hand, and gave a lopsided smile. Why the thought had not crossed her own mind was beyond her. Evidently, having a Companion who could fly would be much more interesting than just having a mount.

"You would do that? That would be wonderful!"

Twilight dipped his head in a bow. "*It would be my great pleasure! I will be able to have us to Valamar before sunset.*"

"Then let us be off!"

Alynniel quickly readied her small pack, and with *Wythring, Angil*, and *Falorn* secure, leapt to the Mahur's back, just behind the wings growing from his shoulders.

The Elfess tangled her hands in Twilight's thick, heavy mane, as with a powerful thrust of his wings he shot up into the air. It was one of the most exhilarating things she had ever experienced. They soared up over the remaining crags of the Graden Hills, and even higher until from the ground they must have appeared as only a large bird in flight. Alynniel decided that it would be very easy to get used to flying. A sudden updraft, though, caused her to tighten her grip with both hands and knees.

"*Worry not, Alynniel,*" Twilight spoke back over his shoulder. "*You are most safe. Anyone I wish to carry need have no fear of falling.*"

Alynniel relaxed her hold somewhat. It was not that she did not believe the Mahur, but looking down at the small patches that were stands of timber or villages on the plains far below kept her from feeling completely secure.

Twilight looked back over his shoulder at the Elfess with what could be taken for nothing but a smirk. Suddenly, he flew in a loop, becoming completely upside-down at the top, then he spiraled down towards a grassy hilltop below. At the last possible second, he swooped back up, into the low-flying clouds, then settled back into a steady flight pattern.

"*Do you believe me now?*" he asked, once again looking back at his passenger.

"Oh please, do that again!"

The Mahur took that to mean yes, gave a happy nicker, and proceeded to carry her through several more sets of loops and dives. Alynniel laughed with pure joy, and raised her hands up into the air over her head. Nothing else she had experienced in her nearly three centuries of life had come close to this feeling of flight.

The Companions took their nooning on a grassy hilltop overlooking the plains. Alynniel enjoyed the rest, and took the opportunity to watch some of the herd animals she could see below. Several farms were also within her view, and she surveyed the patchwork of fields and pens. Men lived so much differently from Elves. The more she observed them, the more intrigued she became.

The sun was slowly sliding past its peak as they once again mounted into the air. The afternoon was filled with delightful soars and swoops, and, as the sun began to sink behind the peaks to the West, the pair was able to make out the gardens and courts of fair Valamar in the foothills below.

Alynniel directed Twilight to a large garden, a fountain bubbling at its center, near the halls of Indariel. As they landed, one of the court guards rushed forward to greet them,a look of wonder on his face at the sight of the Mahur.

"Welcome to Valamar, my lady Alynniel," he said with a slight bow. "The Lady Indariel awaits you in her private chambers. You may leave your . . . mount . . . here in the courtyard.

The Elfess dismounted, and moved forward to embrace the Mahur's arched neck.

"This is Twilight, my Companion," she spoke to the awestruck Elf before her.

She paused and turned to Twilight as he whinnied a question. Looking back to the guardian, she said, "Twilight is both hungry and thirsty. He asks if he may drink from this fount, then graze on the sward nearby."

"He-he asks?" the Elf stuttered in bewilderment. Quickly pulling himself back up into the proper stance becoming a guardian of Valamar, he continued. "But of course. He will be most welcome to do so."

His composure nearly left him once more when Twilight gave him a small bow, then proceeded to the fount to slake his thirst.

"Will you follow me, my lady?"

After giving Twilight a parting smile, Alynniel followed her guide into the grand halls of Valamar. The young Elfess barely took notice of the beautiful surroundings. Multi-hued marble walls and glowing gemstone-colored crystals failed to catch her attention. Tapestries and sculptures she had enjoyed on past visits were ignored. Everything around her seemed to fade and be lost in a mist. Her anticipation caused her total focus to be on the arched double doors at the far end of the hall leading to Indariel's private chambers with the two guards flanking them. Through that portal she hoped to find the answers she had been seeking for so long.

At last they reached their goal. The guards saluted, and opened the wide carved doors as, with a bow, Alynniel's guide bid her enter. The Elfess started to rush forward, but caught herself. Closing her eyes, she took several deep breaths, hoping by sheer will to restore the small quantity of patience she possessed before entering. Having accomplished this to some degree, she stepped forward.

Never having been inside Indariel's private chambers before, Alynniel took just a moment to allow her senses to drink in her surroundings. The perfume of mountain laurel and honeysuckle filled the room. The sound of flowing water and gentle breezes calmed the soul. The floors were of the whitest marble, inlaid with mosaics of flowers and vines. The conversation areas on either side of the room were carpeted with rich woven rugs that looked more like tapestries than floor coverings. The one on the left, when entering the doors, had a bubbling fountain at its heart, while the one on the right had an open fire pit that burned brightly. The walls on the two sides of the room were a series of arches made from a light, cool blue marble. Each of these enclosed beautiful painted scenes and lovely, delicate statues of woodland and mountain creatures that were so life-like Alynniel half expected to see them leap into the room. In the four corners of the room, pillars carved to look like tree trunks rose to the ceiling where their carved branches stretched out to each other and intertwined, trunks, branches, and leaves all carved from the same white marble as the floor. From the ceiling, at seeming random intervals, descended wrought silver vines with golden leaves the end of each holding a crystal lamp of sapphire, amethyst, or emerald.

The room was nearly twice as wide as it was long, and the entire back wall was a bay window of magnificent crystal panes extending up to form a domed skylight over a raised dais. In the center of the back wall on this dais, seeming to meld into both, was a crystal throne. Wall, skylight, and throne all glowed dimly with the light from outside.

"Do you like my Chamber of Seeing?"

Alynniel's eyes were drawn to a beautiful, seemingly ageless Elfess standing to one side of the throne, her jewel-toned robes embroidered with both silver and gold, blending in perfect harmony with the room around her. Her hair hanging long and straight down her back was a lovely, silvery white, her eyes were a clear, pale sky blue, and on her brow rested a crown carved of the same crystal the throne was formed from.

Alynniel made a slow turn, once more taking in the entire room.

"It is wondrous!" she said in a hushed tone as her eyes came back to rest on the Lady Indariel.

The Lady descended from the dais and beckoned Alynniel towards a pair of plush chairs to one side near the fountain.

As soon as they were seated, seeming to sense her guest's eagerness, Indariel began to speak. "I sent for you, Alynniel, because of a vision I received on the Seat of Seeing." She gestured to the throne beside them.

"I saw your journey and the path you needed to take to get here. I also was given to see that you have a very important part to play in the future of Aaleria.

"Before I can tell you more of my vision, you must tell me of any strange or peculiar things that may have happened on your way to me. The Seat of Seeing gives glimpses, but seldom does it reveal the whole truth even to me."

Alynniel leaned slightly forward in her seat. She proceeded to tell Indariel of all that had happened, starting with her curiosity of the Race of Man, to exploring the farm, helping the hunter, and then meeting and rescuing Twilight from the dragon trap.

As she finished her tale, the elder Elfess laid a hand gently on her arm and asked: "Was there not some other happening? Something you could not explain, no matter how small it may have seemed?"

Alynniel went over her journey once more in her mind, then slowly spoke. "There was one thing, but it seemed so small I had forgotten. One night, as I lay down to rest, I thought I saw a blue glow on my arms as I closed my eyes. When I opened them again, there was nothing, so I took it to be imagining."

"Where were you in your journey then?" the Lady asked.

"I was on a hill, perhaps halfway across the land of Smead, overlooking a large keep on the plains below. I had the strangest feeling the entire time I was in that land. A feeling I can no more describe to you now than I could to myself then. Just a feeling of heaviness or disquiet. Like a change in the air before a storm, only different."

Indariel rose and went to the Seat of Seeing. She sat there quietly, her eyes closed for several minutes. The rising moon shining through the crystal caused the glow of the throne and the bay window to increase ever so slightly.

"Come child, you must join me here. The Time of the Moon is quickly approaching."

Alynniel rose to do as she was bidden. As she seated herself on the ample throne slightly facing Indariel, the Lady half turned to face her as well, and took both Alynniel's hands in her own.

"Now, close your eyes, relax, and think on the feeling you had in the land of Smead."

The young Elfess could feel the impatience rising within herself, but forced it down and did as she was bidden. The Moon had risen over the rocks and trees surrounding the halls of Valamar until now it was directly over the Chamber of Seeing. Its light caused both the throne and Indariel's crown to glow more and more brightly until multi-colored beams of light filled the Chamber, bouncing from crystal to crystal around the entire room. Suddenly, there was a burst of white light, then the room faded back to its original soft glow.

Alynniel gave a small gasp and opened her eyes as Indariel released her hands.

"What did you see, my child?"

"I saw myself in many times and many places. In the land of Smead. In the far North. In a vast Swamp. At a Tower pulsing with Evil.

"Most often I was surrounded by Men. Sometimes male, sometimes female, other times both. On many occasions there were one or more of our people present, a few times Dwarves, but almost always there were Men--and there were many battles. Sometimes, I was alone."

Taking a deep breath, she went on. "Each time I envisioned Smead, I saw a Man, though I perceived not his face. I saw what appeared to be a golden cord binding him to me. Much like an Elven wedding cord, though surely that cannot be."

Alynniel rose from the Seat and started pacing back and forth.

"What does it all mean?" she asked as she stopped and looked to the Lady, her hands spread in entreaty. "It makes no sense to me!"

Indariel's soft voice worked as a calming balm to Alynniel's troubled spirit. "Added to mine, your vision shows the path your life will take."

The younger Elfess dropped to her knees at the Lady's feet, much like an eager child would, to hear what the Lady might say.

"Of what you have seen, and what I am to reveal, you must never speak. The wrong word to the wrong person or at the incorrect time could change the course of events and bring terrible consequences." Indariel held the younger Elfess' gaze with her own. "Do I have your solemn promise that you will speak of this to no one, not even Telorin, your father?"

With a serious look, Alynniel slowly dipped her head in a bow of acquiescence. Indariel then continued.

"Your life will be joined to the world of Men. You will aid them in a desperate struggle, in a great conflict against a terrible Evil. You will bring them help when it is most greatly needed, not only by your presence but also through the allies you will find along the way–as you did your Mahur Companion. The events you will accomplish both with their help and on your own. These allies may often be unlooked for, but you must never turn away from offered help, no matter what the circumstance.

"In all of this, the kingdom of Smead will play a great part, as will the Man you saw in your vision. Your paths will cross ever and anon throughout this coming War. This was the cause of both the feeling you had while journeying through Smead, and also the blue glow. The glow was *Lureliare* attempting to show you a possible step upon your path." She paused, the hint of a smile touching the corner of her lips. "As unlikely as it may seem, the golden cord you saw is indeed an Elven wedding cord. It is binding you to this Man of Smead, whom you will wed."

A look of shock passed over Alynniel's face, and Indariel's hand on her shoulder stopped her as she attempted to rise from her place by the Seat.

"Now that I know my path, I must start on my quest! Hold me not here. I must return to Smead! If this be true, I would look upon this Man I am to wed!"

The Lady did not release her hold, but calmly began to speak. "My child, you have found your path, and you will start your quest when you leave this place. But there is yet more I must tell you. The things you have seen and those I have revealed to you are not all in the near future. Some will come to pass before many seasons have come and gone. With others, it is not so. You must not attempt to discover all, but you must allow each event to come at its own pace and time. These events have not all yet been set, and actions of both you and others can alter them.

"As for looking on the Man you will wed. This you cannot do at present, for he has yet to be born."

Alynniel's eyes filled with questions as she gazed up at Indariel. The Lady gently squeezed her shoulder as she said, "The young noble who will be his grandfather is yet a small boy in the courts of Smead. The lives of Men are but a passing breath compared to the life of an Elf. Many things must come to pass on Aaleria before you reach that step in your journey."

As Indariel removed her hand from Alynniel's shoulder, the young Elfess slowly rose from the floor and moved back towards the fountain. She stood there, gazing at it unseeingly, trying to comprehend all that she had learned. Then it was almost as if each splash of the fountain washed her path clearer in her mind. The long hours spent with bow, sword, and shield now had a greater purpose than at first had been evident. She would need all of her great skill to aid in the battle against the Evil that was coming to Aaleria. Even the way she had been drawn towards the world of Man was more understandable now.

As this last thought fell into place, Alynniel's head snapped up, and she spun around to face Indariel once more, a look of chagrin upon her lovely face.

"Two generations of Man before I meet the one I am to wed?! I will never make it!"

About the Authors

C. K. Deatherage earned her B. A. and M. A. from Southern Illinois University at Edwardsville in English and her Ph.D. from Purdue University in Old and Middle English Language and Literature. Her previous publications include *Waysmeet: Poems and Tales of Fantasy and Wonder*, "Niall MacDonaugh and the Leipreachan" in *The RudderHaven Science Fiction and Fantasy Anthology I*, "Final Entry" in *Star Trek: Strange New Worlds V*, and various poems in anthologies and journals. She won the 2013 Poet of the Year and the 2013 Vardis Fisher Award for Most Humorous Piece by the Idaho Writers League. She currently resides in Idaho with her husband, two kids, two large dogs, and four cats—and an occasional very temporary field mouse.

Becca Lynn Rudder is teen-aged girl with a dream of writing a story—and actually finishing one, finally. She is the daughter of Douglas and Sheri Rudder, both of which are also *RudderHaven* authors. They, as well as other members of her family, helped her with the polishing phases of her story. She knows that she couldn't have finished it without their help. Becca lives in southern Illinois with her parents and their dog, Shadow Star. She enjoys MMOs and PC games, movies and TV shows (especially older ones), reading, and just plain talking. She likes Barbies and Princesses—and *really* likes super-heroes, Star Trek/Star Wars, and Lord of the Rings as well. Becca is a young, devoted Christian girl. She actively goes to church. She helps with Junior Church, sings with the choir, and even leads the singing during her grandfather's Bible studies. Most of all, she yearns and loves to follow her LORD and Savior, Jesus Christ.

Douglas Rudder resides in southern Illinois, where he often battles Orcs, Aliens, and Super-Villains with his wife and daughter. A recipient of two English degrees (B.A./M.A.), he is currently an XML data architect (go figure), dwelling in a shadowy corner cubicle he calls the Bat Cave. He is also a general partner and managing editor for RudderHaven. His previous publications include *Tolkien: Roncevaux, Ethandune, and Middle-earth* and short stories in *The RudderHaven Science Fiction and Fantasy Anthology I.* Favorite science fiction and fantasy authors include J. R. R. Tolkien, Robert Heinlein, Timothy Zahn, Jonathan Rudder, and Michael Stackpole, among others. Doug is active in his church as Music Director and soloist, and his whole family is involved in the children's ministries, often writing their own material. He and his family also like to create and play their own home grown RPGs (superhero, fantasy, and science fiction).

Sheri Lynn Rudder, a fortunate stay at home wife and mother, grew up in rural, southeast Iowa. Thanks to her mother and grandfather, she learned at an early age that the best place to find adventures was in books. Almost twenty-four years ago, when she married her knight-in-shining-armour (known to most as Douglas) she was introduced to the wonderful worlds of sci-fi and fantasy, mainly through the writings of JRR Tolkien, Michael

Stackpole, and Timothy Zahn. Now, with her husband's encouragement and the quick-clicking editing pen of her teenage daughter, she is trying her hand at sharing her adventures with you. Sheri is involved in the children's and ladies' ministries at her church, which helped her start writing short stories. She also enjoys the time she spends battling through the different worlds (MMO and RPG) that she shares with her husband and daughter, along with any extended family who wish to tag along.

B. David Spicer lives in Ohio, where he earned a B. A. in English from Ohio University. He has always been an avid reader and one day woke up and started writing fiction of his own. Along with crime fiction, science fiction and horror fiction he'll occasionally jot down a prose poem or two, though he'll probably deny that in court. He sometimes writes scripts for independent comic book publishers, but short stories are his favorite subjects. He likes board and role-playing games and attending gaming conventions.

Paula Welker grew up in Southeastern Missouri, and has spent her adult life in St. Louis. She has a wide variety of interests. She earned a Bachelor of Science in Pharmacy and a Master of Theological Studies. She loves teaching her two piano students, and also enjoys snow skiing with her family. She likes Star Trek and Cardinals baseball, J.R.R. Tolkien and Arthur Conan Doyle, period mysteries and the lives of the saints. She has been writing fantasy stories since she was a teenager, and is excited to finally see one of her worlds in print

CPSIA information can be obtained
at www.ICGtesting.com
Printed in the USA
FFOW03n1628160914
7384FF